REVENGE

SWEET AS CAIN

A Novella by

D.A. Kelley

D1280362

Beloved, never avenge yourselves, but leave it to the wrath of God, for it is written, vengeance is mine, I will repay, says the Lord. (Romans 12:19...ESV)

***

Chapter One

"NOOOO, GET AWAY FROM ME. I AM NOT A WHORE!!!" Elissa screamed and bolted up out of her sleep in a cold sweat. She was having the reoccurring nightmare she'd been having since she was a child, but this time, something was different. There was another person in the dream who hadn't been there before. The person, whoever it was, was a mere silhouette, which made it difficult for her to make out their identity.

The effect adoption had on a person could be outright devastating. The possibilities were endless, accommodated with a broad spectrum of behavioral responses. You never knew which end you would find yourself if that were the fate card you were dealt. You'd either be content with being adopted and it never bothered you, or you would be the one who just couldn't seem to come to grips with the fact your biological parents wanted nothing to do with you. The latter was the case for cardiologist, Dr. Elissa Crystal Johnson.

Elissa found out at an early age she was adopted. Her adoptive parents made it clear she really didn't belong to them. They claimed all they knew about her biological mother was that she was a young girl, not even eighteen years old. In their self-righteous, judgmental eyes, that proved she was a whore. They tried to convince Elissa regardless of who her mother was, either way, she was better off with them. Elissa was repeatedly reminded of how grateful she should be to them for taking her into their home.

Her adoptive mother, Bernice, wasn't really all that bad, but she was under the thumb of her husband, Clifford, and that hindered her from treating her like a daughter. Clifford and Bernice

Johnson were strict churchgoers, who would make anyone not want to ever step foot inside of a church again once you were grown. Although, Elissa viewed them as hypocrites. She'd often questioned how one spent that much time in church, as they had, and still didn't treat people right. Along with the question, she wondered why they had even adopted her since it was obvious they didn't love her. They never treated her like a daughter. Often, they ignored her, and she felt like a tenant in her own home instead of a member of the family.

She'd never forget one Thanksgiving when she was ten years old, the Johnsons had family and friends over for dinner. Elissa was forced to stay in her room. She heard everyone downstairs, laughing and having a good time. She even heard the voice of a young girl, who sounded to be around her age. Although that wasn't what really caught Elissa's attention. The weird thing was the girl's voice strangely resembled Elissa's. Hearing the young girl was like hearing herself speak. If children were invited, why couldn't she join the festivities?

She became so angry, she decided she was going downstairs anyway. Elissa sprung up from her bed and made a short sprint from her bed to the door. When she turned the doorknob, she remembered the warning and stayed put in her room as commanded. The Johnsons had threatened that if she left her room, they wouldn't feed her for a week. That was just one of the many memories, or better yet, nightmares, Elissa had as a child. Sadly, there were plenty more where that came from.

Family functions, she wasn't allowed to participate in or even show her face. Elissa was threatened and forced to remain in her room whenever the Johnsons had company. She simply hated her biological parents for giving her away. Elissa hated them even more for putting her in a position to grow up in such horrible conditions. She tried to get past the feeling of abandonment, but the harder she tried, the stronger the feeling of rejection grew. She promised herself to get the best education and be successful. This promise included getting as far away from Clifford and Bernice as possible. The vow also entailed finding her parents and making them pay for the hard childhood she'd endured. She couldn't shake the feeling that if she'd remained with her real parents, she wouldn't have gone through so much heartache as a child.

Dr. Elissa Johnson accomplished everything she set out to do. At thirty years old, she was one of the top, most sought after cardiologists in New York, but there was still one thing left unfinished. She wasn't one hundred percent sure how she was going to carry everything out, but one thing she was one hundred percent sure about was it was time for…REVENGE!!

Chapter Two

Clifford and Bernice Johnson had long since moved out of New York and relocated to Georgia. The day they left, Elissa couldn't have been happier if she'd won the lottery for millions. Bernice attempted to keep in touch, but Elissa didn't want to be bothered. Although the Johnsons had no qualms about telling her she was adopted, they still never revealed to her who her biological parents were. She was sure they knew, and pondered why they had kept that piece of vital information from her. She often wondered what the big deal was. It would have made her search a little easier had they just told her, but that still didn't stop her mission. She just had to find other means to get the information.

Elissa had faith and knew she would come up with something. She tried her hand at adoption agencies, but it always led to a dead end. It was thirty years ago, and the record keeping wasn't as advanced and accurate as it was today. Elissa still remained focused and determined. She came to the conclusion that she was intelligent. She was a doctor, therefore, surely her brain would figure something out. She considered hiring a private detective but then thought better of it. If she had hit a dead end, she assumed they would, too, and that was when it hit her. The idea was obvious and simple. It was one of those *in plain sight* type deals. She would just go back to her old neighborhood and ask questions.

Elissa sat in the brown leather chair in her office at the hospital, deep in thought. She composed a list of questions she would ask her former neighbors when she went to visit her old neighborhood. She hadn't been back in years. She didn't even know who still lived there, but she was going to soon find out.

She wrote down a list of questions because she didn't want to forget anything. In the middle of writing, she paused and stared at the notepad, and the pen in her hand. Something as simple as the act of *writing* triggered a flashback. She recalled the time she got caught chewing gum in church. Clifford spanked her with a wooden paddle, which had her name carved into it, along with the phantom verse, *Spare the rod and spoil the child.* Elissa remembered thinking, with all the churching and reading the Bible he did, he still didn't know that verse was *not* in the Bible.

The paddle resembled a poor man's version of the cat o' nine tails. A whip the Roman soldiers used for punishment, which was also used to whip Jesus. The nine, twelve-inch thick strips of leather didn't have pieces of metal tied to the ends like a real cat o' nine tails, but he had tied thick knots at the end of each leather strip and stapled them to the paddle. Clifford had crafted the punishment tool from his old leather belts that he no longer wore. She recalled that was one of the many beatings which made it difficult for her to sit down for a week. He also made her write, 'I will not chew gum in church' three thousand times.

She angrily threw the pen on her desk, crumbled up the piece of paper, and entered her questions onto the notepad app on her cell phone instead. She hated that incidents from her childhood constantly popped into her head and had such a negative effect on her.

The drive from Mt. Sinai Hospital in Manhattan, to the old neighborhood in Long Island, didn't seem that long. Maybe her anxiety had pre-occupied her thoughts and shortened the trip in her mind.

She turned down her old block and wasn't sure where to begin, so she started at Mrs. Green's house. Mrs. Green was Bernice's closest friend; they talked about everything. Elissa was sure she would know some useful information. If she were lucky, she would get all she needed from Mrs. Green, and leave the neighborhood once and for all, with no need to ever return.

It was a warm, sunny day, and Mrs. Green was piddling around in her garden when Elissa pulled up. She stepped out of her black Benz SUV and glanced over at her old house, her stomach instantly doing flips. She recalled when she was only fourteen. Elissa was outside, talking to one of the neighborhood boys who attended their church. Clifford ran out of the house like it was on fire and told her to get inside and stop being so fresh. All the kids, and everyone else who was outside, stopped what they were doing, and focused on the scene Clifford was causing at her expense. She was so embarrassed by his actions, all she could do was run in the house in tears.

While inside, he scolded her and said she was going to be just like her mother: a whore. She didn't know what he meant by that. How did they know her mother was *really* all that bad? After all, having a baby as a teenager didn't necessarily make you a whore, which was all the information her parents claimed to know. Clifford's statement sounded like he knew more than he had let on.

Elissa shook the memory from her mind and

continued toward Mrs. Green's home. Mrs. Green rose from her garden when she realized Elissa was walking in her direction. At first, she didn't recognize her, but as Elissa drew closer, a look of recognition was in Mrs. Green's eyes. Elissa extended a polite greeting. Mrs. Green hugged Elissa and told her it was good to see her again. She invited her inside, and they took a seat on the floral couch in the living room. Elissa wasted no time getting to the point of her visit.

"Mrs. Green, I hate to pop up like this," Elissa began, "but I have questions I hope you're able to answer."

Mrs. Green fidgeted with a piece of mail that was lying on the end table.

"You know, I just got off the phone with your mother," Mrs. Green said, or better yet, rambled. Elissa could tell she was trying to avoid something, but what was it? Now she was more anxious than ever to get any information Mrs. Green knew.

"Well, speaking of my mother, that's why I'm

here."

"What about her?"

"I'm not going to beat around the bush with you. Do you know who my real parents are?"

Silence hung in the air, and Elissa held her breath as she waited for Mrs. Green's answer. Elissa decided to plead her case since it seemed Mrs. Green needed some nudging. She explained to her she knew she was adopted, but she really needed to know who her real parents were in order to have closure and peace in her life. Mrs. Green hesitated a while longer, then she spoke.

"First of all, you need to know your mother loves you very much, and she's proud of you. When I say mother, I'm talking about Bernice."

Elissa found that very hard to believe, but since Mrs. Green had started talking, she didn't want to interrupt her flow, so she kept her opinion to herself.

Mrs. Green continued, "Clifford and Bernice are really your great uncle and aunt. Your mother is their niece. Clifford and your biological mother's father are brothers."

Elissa sat there with her mouth opened, literally. She was more upset now to know Clifford was her blood relative, and he had still treated her like she was nothing. Elissa couldn't believe it. She felt anger envelop her like she'd never felt before. The feeling was so strong, it scared her.

"Do you know anything else about my mother? My *real* mother," she questioned, her voice trembling.

"Bernice didn't tell me everything, but I do know your mother and your grandparents lived somewhere in Queens. Your grandparents' names are Henry and Charlotte Johnson. That's all I know."

Elissa stood, her legs almost giving out on her, and she slightly stumbled. Mrs. Green reached out to help her, but Elissa regained her footing. She thanked Mrs. Green for her help and headed toward the door.

Mrs. Green and Bernice were close friends, but she never cared too much for Clifford. He didn't treat Elissa right when she was growing up, and she took this as an opportunity to try and make things right. She kindly asked Elissa not to tell Bernice about their conversation. Elissa replied she no longer communicated with her parents. She gave Mrs. Green her business card, just in case something else came to mind, and she wanted to call her. Mrs. Green graciously took the card and placed it in the pocket of her house dress. Elissa thanked her again and walked out.

If she had considered letting her vendetta go, that option was no longer on the table. To know the people who called themselves her parents, were actually her real family and had treated her so cruelly sprinkled sugar on the situation and made her decision for revenge taste that much sweeter.

Chapter Three

Elissa lounged in a chair on the patio of her penthouse condo in midtown Manhattan, in her bright-colored, floral maxi dress and huge sunglasses that covered a great portion of her face, trying to come up with a master plan. Honestly, she really hadn't planned on getting revenge on Clifford and Bernice. As far as they were concerned, she just wanted to get out of their house and have nothing else to do with them in life, but with this newfound information about them being family, she couldn't shake the feeling of wanting to get them back, too.

Every time she thought about how she had the same blood coursing through her veins as Clifford, and he still treated her like an outsider, she saw red. She recalled the many times he referred to her as a whore, whenever he thought the label suited her. She was hot with anger, and that was when the idea hit her.

When Elissa was a child, she kept a journal of

all the mean and terrible things Clifford and Bernice had done to her. The journal was a form of therapy. It allowed her to release her anger onto paper instead of onto them because, when it boiled down to it, Elissa had murder on her heart. She'd lost count of the times she'd contemplated getting up in the middle of the night and killing them in their sleep, or setting the house ablaze with both of them still inside. The only thing that kept them alive was the verse in the Bible that read, *Thou shall not kill,* but maybe it was time for her journal to become a bestseller. She'd work the details out later, but it was time to get this revenge show on the road.

Elissa informed the hospital she was going to be out for a couple of days. She didn't have many friends, but that was solely by choice. Thanks to her parents, or better yet, great aunt and uncle, Elissa didn't trust many people. She firmly believed if you couldn't trust your *parents,* then who could you trust? She did have one person she considered a friend, and everyone else was associates, if that.

Dr. Ann McCoy was a colleague she had met at a three-day medical conference that was held in New York a few years ago. She and Ann clicked instantly, although Elissa had always thought their encounter was kind of odd. Out of all the people in attendance, it was as if Ann had handpicked her as the one she wanted to get to know. It was during the meet and greet portion of the conference, and everyone was introducing themselves and exchanging business cards. Elissa was in the middle of a conversation with a pediatrician when she spotted an older lady maneuvering through the crowd. It didn't take long for Elissa to realize the woman was making her way over to her. She reached Elissa just as the pediatrician walked away. She was an attractive older woman, but not old enough to be considered elderly.

"Hi, my name is Dr. Ann McCoy." She extended a well-manicured hand.

"Hello, nice to meet you. My name is Dr. Elissa Johnson."

"Is this your first time attending one of these events?"

"This is the first one I've attended in New York," Elissa responded in a friendly tone.

"So, what is your specialty?" Ann questioned.

"Cardiology."

"Well, isn't that a coincidence. I'm a cardiologist as well."

They engaged in small talk, and Elissa found it very easy to converse with Ann. It felt like she'd known her for years. Over the course of the three days, they got to know each other better. Elissa learned Ann had been happily married for twenty-five years to a man she'd met in college. She had a son who was twenty years old, and also a daughter who had twin girls who were ten years old. Elissa couldn't put it into words what she felt, but she felt a strong connection to Ann, and when the conference was over, they were sure to exchange phone numbers and email addresses so they could keep in touch. Ann also lived in New York, and her private practice wasn't too far from the hospital where Elissa worked. They agreed to do lunch from time to time.

Elissa dialed Ann's home number, and a man answered the phone. She assumed it was her husband. Elissa could tell he was preoccupied because as soon as she extended her greeting, he responded with a quick hello and told her to hang on. He must have laid the phone down and walked away because his voice seemed far away when he called out for Ann, but she thought she heard him say *Jalissa* was on the phone. She heard Ann yell that she had the phone, and the man hung up.

"Heyyyy, baby," Ann sang into the receiver.

"Hey to you, too," Elissa replied, smiling.

"Oh, hi, Elissa," Ann repeated, this time as if they hadn't already greeted each other.

"Was that your husband who answered the phone?"

"Yeah, that was him."

"Tell him my name is E-lissa, not Ja-lissa," she chuckled.

"Wh-what do you mean by that?" Ann questioned with tension in her voice.

Elissa looked at the phone and furrowed her brow as if Ann was able to see her facial expression. She wondered why all of a sudden, she'd gotten so serious.

"Oh, nothing, just that I heard him say Ja-lissa was on the phone."

Ann chuckled to lighten the mood. "Oh, you know how men are. If it's not ESPN, they're not really paying attention."

"Well, I'm just calling to let you know I'm taking an impromptu vacation. I will call you when I return."

"Okay, be safe, and be sure to call me when you get back so we can catch up."

The women hung up, and Elissa retrieved her luggage from the coat closet and started packing.

She wouldn't be gone long, so the smaller suitcase would do just fine. She really didn't feel like making that drive to Georgia. She would have rather flown, but she was packing some things that would not have made it past airport security, so driving was the safest choice.

Chapter Four

Elissa decided to leave bright and early the following morning. She set the alarm on her cell phone for 5:00 a.m. It didn't take long for her to get past the toll booths, and once that was completed, she headed in the direction of Georgia. The skies were blue from state to state, which made the drive a little more relaxing, despite all the hours it would take to get to Georgia. She decided to do a one-way car rental, figuring she would fly back after she left her mark in Georgia.

When she finally arrived in Georgia, she was extremely tired and exhausted. She checked in at the Marriott in Downtown Atlanta. She was sleepy and hungry, but sleep took precedence. She retrieved her suite key from the clerk and crashed as soon as her body felt the soft mattress, and her head hit the fluffy pillows.

Elissa rose early the next morning, anxious to get things rolling. Although she wasn't a frequent churchgoer, she usually prayed in the mornings.

Considering the nature of this trip, she didn't feel comfortable praying, so she simply thanked God for waking her up.

She took a long, hot shower. The wide spa showerhead with six settings transformed the simple shower into a liquid massage session. She made a mental note to purchase a spa showerhead when she returned to New York.

The location Elissa was going to was in Buckhead, and according to the front desk clerk, that wasn't too far from the hotel. Atlanta traffic was worse than New York's if you asked Elissa, but she finally pulled up to the address she had entered into her GPS, and she couldn't believe her eyes. She re-checked to make sure she'd entered the correct address into her navigational system. The neighborhood could easily be featured in a magazine doing a spread on upscale homes in affluent areas. Just gazing up at the extravagant home stoked a memory.

Elissa reminisced about the time she told her

parents she really needed a new pair of sneakers for gym because the ones she had no longer fit. They retorted they didn't have the money, as always. She bugged them and begged them until they finally flat out said no. To add insult to injury, a week later, Elissa realized they had a brand new, thirty-two-inch television in their bedroom. Clifford always claimed not to have money when she needed something, only to later buy something he wanted. Clifford's reply was he was only obligated to clothe, feed, and give her shelter, buying her *extra* things were not part of the deal. *What deal?* she always thought.

Her mind continued to drift. One day after gym class, Elissa hung around after all the girls had dressed and left the locker room. She frantically checked all the lockers that didn't have combination locks on them. She rummaged through the section of lockers the freshmen used since she was a sophomore and didn't mingle with freshmen students. Elissa inspected ten lockers before she stumbled upon what she was looking for. She silently asked God to forgive her and stuffed the size seven black classic Reeboks in her gym bag and ran out of the locker room.

Elissa continued to admire the mini-mansion she was parked in front of. She wasn't jealous because her career as a doctor afforded her to live in luxury as well. The feeling she felt was more shock and resentment, if anything. All this time, they were sitting on this type of money, and they couldn't buy her a twenty-five dollar pair of sneakers, she concluded. She immediately became infuriated again.

* * *

Her game plan was to stake out in the neighborhood in order to learn Clifford's and Bernice's daily routine and schedule. They were pretty basic and stuck to their routine, so she anticipated the process would take only two days. She was correct in her theory. For two days, she parked across the street, down the block, and noted they were out of the house by 8:30 a.m. and they were back home no later than 6 p.m.

Elissa devised her strategy, and all she had to do now was put it into action. The night before, she made sure she had everything she needed. The third day had finally arrived, and Elissa spent the first half of the day shopping since her plan wasn't scheduled to go into motion until later that evening. It seemed to take forever for 5:00 p.m. to strike on the clock. She was constantly checking the time. She felt like a kid at Christmas, waiting for Santa to come.

Elissa pulled up to the lavish home and parked the rental in the back so no one would know she was there. She stepped out of the car and trotted up to the back door, which was the entrance to an outdoor sunroom. Luckily, the door was unlocked, not that it really mattered. Elissa was prepared to break in, either by attempting to pick the lock, or breaking a window, but she'd assumed one of the doors would be unlocked in this fancy area. It was apparent burglary was not high on the list around these parts.

The glass double doors she entered led directly to the dining area. She glanced around and couldn't help but acknowledge that the room alone could have easily been featured in *Better Homes & Gardens*. Elissa wanted to trash the place for no real reason at all, but that wasn't part of the agenda, so she took a tour while she waited. Elissa scrolled through their caller ID on the house phone and stored numbers in her cell phone she thought might come in handy later on. From the caller ID, she had the numbers to Clifford's and Bernice's places of employment, and the number to the church they attended, along with the pastor's private home and cell phone numbers.

While touring, what was obviously the master bedroom, she heard voices. *Shoot*, she thought, they were home early. The house was so big, once inside, she couldn't hear what was going on outside, which hindered her from hearing a car pull up. They were coming up the stairs, and she could easily make out Clifford's voice, but the female's voice definitely wasn't Bernice's. Elissa hurriedly hid in the walk-in closet, which was the size of a small bedroom.

Clifford and the woman, who appeared to be around twenty-five years old, entered the room. The woman's whiny voice put Elissa in the mind of a teenybopper. She sounded like a teenaged girl who should be in high school somewhere. Teenybopper whined about him not taking her shopping. Clifford assured her he would spend double on her next week. Teenybopper giggled and was clearly appeased by that offer. Clifford urged her they had to hurry because Bernice would be home soon. Teenybopper wasted no time stripping out of her mini skirt and stilettos, and Clifford swiftly removed his tie and three-piece suit. Elissa's stomach churned as she witnessed the immoral act, and she also recollected the numerous times he'd referred to her as a whore, when evidently, he was the man whore.

Ten minutes later, the deed was done, and Clifford and Teenybopper wasted no time getting dressed. As Clifford escorted Teenybopper out the room, he reminded her to remember to give Bishop Payne his message about finalizing the order for the new sound system at the church. Teenybopper's reply was what threw Elissa for an even further loop.

"Don't worry, Deacon, I'm the secretary, and I'll be sure to give my father the message," she winked and gave him a kiss. Clifford patted her on her backside, and they walked out. Maybe God was on her side, concluded Elissa, because the information she'd just gotten in the last ten minutes was far better than what she had. Elissa smirked as she hatched plan B in her head.

Chapter Five

Fifteen minutes later, and Bernice was home. Elissa was still hiding out in the small bedroom they deemed a closet. There was even a full bathroom attached, so she was comfortable. She was waiting for the right moment and was prepared to wait all night if she had to. Fortunately, it wasn't going to take all night. She heard Bernice yell to Clifford that she would prepare dinner as soon as she changed out of her scrubs, as she climbed the steps.

"BINGO!!" whispered Elissa.

Bernice entered the room and removed her nursing shoes. She sat on the bed and massaged her feet for a few seconds. While humming an old gospel song by James Cleveland, she removed her light blue scrubs and opened the closet to retrieve another outfit. Bernice was greeted with Elissa pointing a .22 caliber handgun directly toward her face. The man at the pawn shop, where Elissa had purchased the gun, told her it was a low caliber gun with low caliber bullets, which had a low deterrent. Elissa didn't want to actually murder them, but she did want to get her point across, so she presumed a low caliber gun was the wisest choice.

Bernice jumped back and wanted to scream, but nothing would come out. She was speechless. Elissa slowly emerged from the closet, still aiming the gun at Bernice. Clifford called up the steps and questioned Bernice about what was taking her so long because he was hungry. When Bernice didn't answer, Clifford marched up the steps to the bedroom. He was halted in his tracks when he saw Elissa pointing the gun at Bernice.

"What's wrong, mom and dad, or should I say, great aunt and uncle? You don't look happy to see me," Elissa hissed.

Clifford and Bernice sneaked a quick peek at each other, as to ask, how did she find out we're really related? The surprised look on their faces confirmed the statement was true. These two were really her aunt and uncle. Somewhere deep inside of her, she wanted it to be a lie because she didn't want to believe someone would actually treat their flesh and blood the way they'd treated her.

"Sit down!!" Elissa shouted as she moved the gun from one to the other.

Bernice sat on the bed and Clifford followed. He possessed a laid back demeanor as if he didn't have a care in the world. Elissa wanted to put a bullet in his leg just to wipe the look off his face, but she had something better in mind that was going to be more effective than a bullet.

"Why are you doing this?" Bernice questioned through tears.

"I'll be the one asking the questions," Elissa retorted.

"What do you want from us?" Clifford chimed in.

"I have a few questions I need you to answer. We can either do this the easy way or the hard way, the choice is up to you."

"What do you want to know?" Bernice asked,

still crying.

"Well, auntie and uncle, for starters, I want information about my real parents."

"We don't know what you're talking about," Clifford lied.

Elissa fired the handgun, and the bullet penetrated the ceiling. Bernice released a high pitched yelp. Clifford shot her an annoyed glare and shook his head in disgust.

"I'm going to ask you one more time. Who are my real parents, and where do they live?"

"Clifford, let's just tell her before somebody gets hurt. It doesn't matter at this point anyway," Bernice pleaded.

"Come on, Bernice, she's just trying to scare us. She's not really going to shoot us," he stated casually.

"He's right, auntie, I wasn't planning on shooting anybody today, but if I have to, I will. But, I'm going to try and play fair," Elissa chuckled.

Elissa retrieved her journal from her oversized

purse and read a few passages.

"Dear Diary,

Today was another, "worst day of my life," which seems to be the story of my life. I got home late today from school because the school bus broke down. As soon as I stepped in the door, my father slapped me and called me a whore. He said he knows I was out fooling around with some boy, and that God was going to punish me."

Elissa continued,

"Dear Diary,

Today was another "feast on spiritual food" day. I don't know how Roger, from my science class, got my number, but he did, and he called me. My mother answered the phone and told him I wasn't allowed to get phone calls. When my father came home, she couldn't wait to tell him. Yep, you guessed it, diary, he called me a whore and said tonight, I had to read the whole book of Revelation in the Bible and write an essay. He said tonight, I was going to feast on spiritual food, and that only meant one thing: I wasn't allowed to have natural food."

She flipped through the pages of the black and white composition notebook that she'd labeled as her diary, looking for another good entry to read.

"Ahhh, here's a good one," she insisted.

"Dear Diary,

I'm writing this in a lot of pain; not just emotional pain, but physical pain. Today, I went to an after-school dance that was held in the gym. Everyone was there, and believe it or not, I had a lot of fun. For a few moments, I felt like a normal fifteen-year-old girl, and it felt good. Even though my mother embarrassed me a couple of weeks ago when Roger called me, he still asked me to dance, and I said yes. It wasn't a slow dance or anything like that. We danced to "No Scrubs" by TLC.

"My father must have some type of digital tracking device attached to me. Immediately, when the dance was over, I spotted him standing at the entrance to the gymnasium. He gestured for me to

come on, with an angry glare plastered on his face. I didn't even know he was coming to pick me up. I told him Monica's mom was going to drop me off at home and he said that would be fine. I think he set me up.

"Anyway, as soon as I got home, he commanded that I go directly to my room. Minutes later, he and my mother barged in my room. He demanded that I read Deuteronomy 25:2-3 out loud. 'If the guilty person deserves to be beaten, the judge shall make them lie down and have them flogged in his presence with the number of lashes the crime deserves, but the judge must not impose more than forty lashes...' After reading that scripture repeatedly, until my father said stop, he called me a whore for dancing with a boy and forced me to lie across the bed on my stomach. He removed his leather belt from the waist of his pants and gave me forty lashes across my back as my mother counted them off. When the beating was over, he expressed once again that was the

punishment for being a whore."

Elissa stopped reading because she felt herself becoming too emotional, and she had to remain in control, so she slammed the journal closed.

"Why were you so… mean?" she shouted. She paused in the middle of her rant because she felt a curse trying to slip through her lips, but she caught herself.

"We're sorry," cried Bernice.

"Your apology means nothing to me now. If you were so sorry, you should have done something. Yeah, maybe you weren't as mean as good old Uncle Clifford here." She pointed the gun in his direction. "But you didn't do anything to stop him, so in my eyes, you're just as guilty."

"We don't owe her anything," shouted Clifford. "We clothed and fed her. We held up our end of the bargain."

Again, Elissa wanted to put a bullet in him, but she remained focused.

"If you don't tell me everything I need to know

42

about my parents and grandparents, I promise you pages of this journal will surface in places you wouldn't like, with your church being one of them."

"And how you plan on doing that? You don't know where our church is."
" Hmmm, you're correct again, Unc, but I'll just call good ole Bishop Payne myself."

Elissa pulled out her cell phone and rambled off the numbers for Bishop Clarence Payne that she'd entered into her phone earlier. Bernice continued to apologize and plead with Elissa, but Elissa had long since turned a deaf ear to her pleas.

"OK, so you have his number. It's not a guarantee he'll believe you. It'll be your word against mine, and I'm well respected in my church."

Elissa ignored him and proceeded to scroll through her phone. Elissa was getting bored with the whole scene and decided to pull out her trump card to end this. Bernice was still crying, and

Clifford was still rambling off at the mouth. Elissa pressed play on her cell phone, and the room got quiet.

"You didn't take me shopping today."

"I'll spend double on you next week."

"We have to hurry, Bernice will be home soon."

"And look, Unc, I even got pictures."

Elissa showed them the video she'd recorded of Clifford and Teenybopper having sex on their bed. Clifford jumped up, and Elissa aimed the gun at his head.

"Please give me a reason to put a bullet in you."

The sinister glare in her eyes let him know she wouldn't hesitate to do just that. Clifford slowly sat back down, and Bernice scooted away from him.

"Now, unless you want Bishop Payne and your entire church to know you're sleeping with his daughter, I suggest you tell me what I want to know."

Bernice and Clifford both admitted she was

really their great niece. Clifford had a brother named Henry Johnson. Henry was married to a woman named Charlotte, and they were her grandparents. They revealed her mother's name was Crystal, but they never knew who her father was. Bernice further explained to Elissa that her mother was only fifteen years old when she had her, and since she couldn't have children, her grandfather suggested she come live with them. Clifford chimed in and said she was born out of wedlock, and that could only mean one thing: her mother was a whore. He expressed God was not pleased with that, and neither was her grandfather. Her grandfather believed in generations paying for the sins of the previous generation, so he made it clear Elissa had to be punished for her mother's sinful act, and being a whore was the worse sin of all in his eyes. Bernice interrupted again and uncovered the fact that her grandparents lived in Bayside, Queens, and her mother had gotten married years ago and was estranged from the family, so they didn't know where she was.

"Okay, you got what you wanted, now get out," demanded Clifford.

"Gladly," replied Elissa.

"Wait a minute, what are you going to do with the video?"

"I'm keeping it for insurance purposes."

"Well, how do I know the video won't go viral?"

Elissa glared directly in his face and exclaimed, "You don't."

Clifford leaped in her direction, as he had attempted to do earlier, but this time, he wasn't so lucky. Elissa pulled the trigger, and the bullet grazed his upper arm. She could have done more damage with the bullet, but she still couldn't find it in her heart to kill him. Grazing him made her feel good, however.

She retrieved a lighter from her bag, lit her journal, and dropped it to the floor. She no longer needed the journal; the video of Clifford and his infidelity suited her just fine. She continued toward the door as Clifford writhed in pain on the floor. Bernice scrambled to put the fire out as well as tried to stop Clifford from bleeding all over their white rug. She was a nurse, so she knew what to do. Although, Elissa didn't see why she would want to help him, with his cheating self.

Elissa glanced back, and if she wasn't mistaken, Bernice was focused more on putting the fire out than helping Clifford. Elissa shot them a smug look and strolled out. She didn't care if the house burned to the ground.

Chapter Six

Elissa had been back in New York for two days, and since returning from Georgia, she'd felt like a different person. She was engulfed by her desire to seek revenge, but also often wondered if she should let it go. She felt justified and vindicated with how she had handled Clifford and Bernice. Maybe that should suffice.

The cops hadn't come knocking on her door, for arson or for shooting Clifford, so maybe she shouldn't look a gift horse in the mouth, whatever that *really* meant, and drop it before things went too far. It wasn't a guarantee that if she continued, she would be as lucky the next time. That was a fleeting thought, because the minute she analyzed the facts, revenge looked better and better.

Instead of dealing with the reality of her birth, her grandparents thought it best to just throw her away like she didn't exist. Yeah, they had kept it all in the family, but what good was that if they weren't going to come around and have a relationship with her? Not to mention, her great aunt and uncle treated her worse than she believed any stranger would have. Elissa was convinced she would have fared better in foster care or with a real adoptive family.

And then there was her mother. Elissa totally understood her mother not being able to raise her because of her age, but what about when she became grown? Why hadn't she come get her? When Elissa took all of that into consideration, revenge seemed to be the only reasonable answer.

Elissa had not yet returned to work. She contemplated again whether to hire a private investigator to locate her mother and grandparents, or just do it herself. She vaguely remembered Ann mentioning growing up in Bayside, or having family in Bayside, something to that effect. She thought about asking her if she knew a Henry and Charlotte Johnson, but then again, that would open a door for questions she wasn't quite ready to answer or a discussion about her personal business she wasn't quite ready to talk about. Elissa opted for the private investigator. She reasoned to at least let him or her do the groundwork, and she'd take it from there.

Elissa headed to the kitchen to pour herself a glass of chilled white wine. She was tense and on edge about finding out more information about her mother. The wine would help her relax. Elissa turned on some jazz music and fired up her laptop to start her search for a good private investigator. She hadn't gotten far into her search before her cell phone interrupted the process. She observed the caller ID screen that read Dr. Ann.

"Heyyyy," she answered.

"Hello, stranger. How was your trip?"

"It was informative, if nothing else."

"I hadn't heard from you, so I was just calling to see if you were back yet."

"My apologies, I meant to call you, I've just had a lot on my plate these past few days."

"Like what? If you don't mind me asking," Ann entreated caringly.

The question gave Elissa pause. She wasn't planning on asking Ann any questions, but maybe this was fate. Since day one, Ann had come off as a person who could be trusted. Due to the age gap between them, she was more of a mother figure than a friend. Elissa decided to give Ann a little more detail than usual. The truth of the matter was, Elissa didn't have anyone to talk to about how she felt except Ann.

In a nutshell, she told Ann she was adopted and that her so-called adoptive parents were really her great aunt and uncle. It dawned on Elissa that she probably wasn't really adopted, not legally, anyway. From the sound of things, her mother had just *given* her away with no paperwork or anything. She revealed to Ann that her aunt and uncle treated her badly and were abusive. Elissa thought she heard Ann sniffle, as if she was crying, but she continued. She ended her tale by telling Ann that, although she knew it wasn't Christian-like, she hated her mother for giving her away, and she would never forgive her — ever!!

"That's awful," Ann responded. "If there's anything I can do, just let me know."

"I do have one question, or maybe two, if you don't mind."

"Sure, sweetie, what is it?"

"Didn't you say you grew up in Bayside, Queens?"

"Yes," Ann supplied the one-word answer. Elissa waited for more of an explanation to follow, but one never came.

"Do you know Henry and Charlotte Johnson?"

Elissa heard a banging noise, which sounded as if Ann's phone had dropped to the floor.

"Ann, Ann!" Elissa called out.

The line was silent for a few more moments, and Ann finally spoke.

"Sorry, the phone just slipped right out of my hand. I'm sorry, Elissa, but I have to go. The twins are over, and they are vying for my attention. Can we finish this conversation later?"

Elissa thought the conversation hadn't really started, but oh well.

"Sure. I have something I need to do anyway. Call me later," Elissa offered.

"Yes, I will," Ann stated.

She hung up before Elissa could say goodbye,

and Elissa stared at the phone for a few lingering minutes, wondering what had gotten into Ann all of a sudden.

Ann remained seated on the edge of her king-sized bed long after the call ended between her and Elissa. Hearing the words Bayside, Queens, and her parents' names, brought back ugly memories, memories she wanted to keep buried, but were slowly making their way to the forefront of her mind, no matter how hard she tried to suppress them. Her mind started to drift, and she was no longer in control of her thoughts. She leaned back onto the bed and, for the first time in a long time, she let the memories come.

***

Crystal Ann Johnson was fifteen years old with a bright and promising future. She made straight A's, and college was definitely in her future. She was determined to go to medical school and become a physician so she could get out of her parents' home as soon as humanly possible… until she met him.

It was the beginning of her sophomore year in high school, and Charles Bradley was the new boy at school. At seventeen years old, all the girls immediately flocked to him and wanted to get to know him better, especially freshmen and sophomores. He was a senior and instantly became the star on the wrestling team. Crystal thought he was cute with his wavy hair and dimples in both cheeks, but she personally thought the behavior of the other girls was pathetic. Although it wasn't fair to Charles at the time, the actions of the others made her not even want to get to know him. There was also something about him that she couldn't put her finger on. Maybe it was his cockiness that made her not want to have anything to do with him. It was apparent he was used to the girls falling all over him, and Crystal refused to be that girl.

She caught him eyeing and smiling at her whenever she walked by in the hallway, but she simply ignored him and did not acknowledge his presence. They did that song and dance for about a month, him trying to get her attention, and her acting like he didn't exist, until the one day she found herself stranded and Charles was the only one around to help her.

Crystal stayed late after school one day for a meeting with the debate team. It was a Friday night, which meant it was church night in her house. Her parents allowed her to participate in extracurricular activities at school, as long as it didn't interfere with her church schedule. Her father was a preacher and had very strict rules. He warned her the first time she missed church due to a school activity, that was going to be the last day of her participating in any events at school.

Her best friend, Lisa, was also on the debate team, and her mother usually dropped her off at home, but Lisa wasn't feeling well and had gone home early, and that left Crystal without a ride. She could have called her father, but that was another rule. Since it was a church night, that meant he was studying the Bible. He made it clear he was not to be disturbed on church days, and that clearly meant not to call him for anything. Even if she called to tell her mother, her mother was sure to tell her father, and that wouldn't be good. She didn't have any money on her for public transportation, and she lived too far from the school to walk home, but walking looked like her only option. She definitely wouldn't make it home in time for church service, so she just came to grips with the fact that was her last day on the debate team, or any other team for that matter. She gathered her things and started to walk home with tears in her eyes.

Crystal had already walked a few blocks when someone honking their horn, got her attention. She ignored the honking without even looking to see who it was. The driver slowed down and rolled down the window on the passenger side of the brown Buick.

"Hey, Crystal, do you want me to take you

home?"

Crystal peered in the car and realized it was Charles. Those dimples jumped out at her, but she didn't want to show any interest.

"No, thank you. I'll walk," she responded with attitude.

"Come on, I just want to take you home, nothing more. You know you don't really want to walk."

He was right, she did have a long walk ahead of her, and truth be told, she'd rather ride than walk. He could tell she was convinced, so he pulled over to the curb and stopped the car. He jumped out and rushed over to the passenger side to open the car door for her. She hesitantly walked toward the car and got in.

Crystal told Charles what street she lived on, and he drove in that direction, but when they were a few blocks away, he pulled the car over into a nearby alley. She was OK with that because she didn't want her father to see her getting out of a stranger's car anyway, but Charles had something else in mind.

"Why are you always playing hard to get?"

"I don't play hard to get, I'm just focused on my school work."

"So why you never speak to me? I know you see me trying to get your attention, but you just ignore me."

"I don't ignore you. You've only been at the school for a month. It's not like we really know each other."

He gazed at her, and his eyes became dark slits. Her father had preached many times about how one could be possessed with an evil spirit, but she had never witnessed it firsthand.

"Well, we could have gotten to know each other by now if you didn't act all stuck up like you're better than somebody."

Panic started to creep in, and all Crystal wanted to do was get out of the car and make it to her house. She figured the best way to do that was to agree with everything he said.

"You're right, but I didn't mean anything by it. We can be friends if you want." She tried to sound calm, but inside, she shook with fear.

"Oh, now you want to be a brotha's friend." It was more of a statement than a question.

"Su-sure, we can be friends," she stuttered, "but I have church tonight. I have to hurry up and get home. I'll see you Monday at school. Thanks for the ride."

Crystal felt like she was rambling, but she was so nervous, and her only goal was to get out of Charles' car safely. She reached for the door handle, and he pounced on her.

"You're not going anywhere until I'm finished with you," he replied with venom in his tone.

Instantly, chaos erupted in the car. Crystal struggled, but she was no match for Charles. He was on the wrestling team, for goodness sakes, how could she ever overpower him?

Crystal screamed, punched, kicked, and

scratched, but that did not faze him. He performed some kind of quick wrestling move, and Crystal found herself in the back seat of the Buick, with him on top of her, pinning her down. When she heard the zipper on his pants and the clanking sound of his belt buckle, she knew what was getting ready to happen. She continued to scream, hoping, or better yet, praying someone would hear her.

Whap! Whap!

The screaming annoyed Charles, mainly because he didn't want someone to eventually hear her, so he slapped her twice across the face and yelled for her to shut up, or else things were going to get a lot worse. She took heed to his threat and stopped screaming. When he raised her skirt and tugged on her underwear, she felt another scream try to escape her lips, but she didn't know what he was capable of, so she kept quiet and let the tears roll down her cheeks. She was a virgin, so he had to force his way inside of her. The rape didn't take long at all, but to Crystal, it felt like forever.

When it was over, Charles opened the back door and pushed her out onto the sidewalk and threw her belongings on the ground next to her. He spat in her direction, and his saliva barely missed her face. He got back into the driver's seat.

"I bet now you'll stop acting like you're too good to speak to somebody," he snapped and pulled off without even a second thought to what he had just done.

Crystal got up off the ground, picked up her things, and straightened out her clothes. She shook uncontrollably, but she had to get herself together before entering the house. It was going to be impossible to cover up the redness in her eyes, which meant she was crying, so she had to come up with a quick lie, just in case she couldn't make it to her room without seeing her parents.

She opened the front door, and there were no parents in sight. She sighed with relief and rushed to her room. As she walked up the steps, she heard her mother call out from their bedroom.

"Crystal, hurry up and get dressed. We're leaving for church in an hour."

"Ma, can I stay home tonight?"

"What you mean, can you stay home?" her father responded with harshness in his voice.

"I'm not feeling well, daddy."

By this time, Crystal was standing at their bedroom door, praying he would say it was okay for her to stay home without opening the door, so she could hurry off to her room without them seeing how awful she looked. That was wishful thinking. Her mother opened the door of their bedroom and was halted in her tracks.

"My God, child, what's wrong with you?" her mother questioned.

"Nothing, Ma. All of a sudden, I started feeling sick. It's probably something I ate at school."

Her father interrupted once again. "Okay, you can stay home this one time since you're not feeling well, but don't make this a habit," he stated, the harshness still in his tone.

Her mother gave her a hug and a kiss on the forehead before they left. Crystal couldn't move fast because of the soreness between her legs. A soreness which reminded her she was no longer a virgin. A soreness which caused her to shuffle to her room with fresh tears falling down her face.

Four months had gone by, and although Crystal felt like she was bigger than the average pregnant woman at this time, she could no longer hide the life that was growing inside of her body. She knew her parents suspected something was different about her from the way she caught them gazing at her at times, but they hadn't approached her. She told her best friend, Lisa, who the father was, but she was too ashamed to tell her he'd raped her. So, Lisa assumed Elissa and Charles had sex willingly, and that was it.

Other than Lisa, no one at school knew she was pregnant, but one could only wear big clothes but so long. Sooner or later, her pregnancy would no longer be a secret. Since Charles had raped her and wasn't really interested in having a relationship with her, he resumed his life like nothing had happened. Every day at school, he laughed it up with his friends like he wasn't a criminal, or to be more precise, a rapist. He no longer tried to get her attention like he'd done in the beginning, and he started treating her like she didn't exist. The tables had turned, but Crystal couldn't care less. She didn't want anything from him, except for him to disappear into thin air. Since her name wasn't Houdini, she didn't see that happening any time soon.

Crystal was a Christian, and she hated to admit it to herself, but she hated Charles, and that was all there was to it. She prayed daily for God to take the hate away, but he hadn't removed it yet, so as of now, she hated him. Truth be told, she was okay with that. She had never reported him to the police. She had willingly gotten in the car with him, so it would be his word against hers, so she just lived with the hate and pain and tried to move on.

One night, while Crystal was sitting in her room, reminiscing about the rape and thinking about how much she hated Charles, as she had done countless times since the incident, she felt a quick flutter in her stomach. Everything she'd ever read came to the forefront of her mind, and from all the books she was secretly reading, she knew the baby had just kicked. She instantly put her hands on her stomach, and at that moment, the hate she had for Charles was replaced with love for her unborn child. The love she suddenly felt overwhelmed her, and nothing else in the world mattered. Crystal decided it was time to tell her parents she was pregnant and face the consequences.

It was a Sunday morning, and Crystal and her parents were on their way out the door, headed to Sunday morning service. Crystal decided that was as good a time as any to break the news, but she didn't know exactly how to start the conversation. Crystal lagged behind as they all marched to the car.

"Put some pep in your step, child," her father called back to her over his shoulder.

Crystal blurted out, "I'm pregnant."

Everyone stopped where they were. It even felt like the earth had stopped.

Well, it's out there now, so let the punishment chips fall where they may, thought Crystal.

Her father whirled around toward her. "What did you just say?"

Her mother stood there, paralyzed. One hand flew over her mouth, and the other hand clutched her imaginary pearls, tears threatening to roll down her face. Her father turned on his heels and stomped back into the house. Crystal and her mother followed. When they were all back in the house, her father repeated what he'd said moments ago.

"What did you just say?"

"I'm pregnant," Crystal repeated with her head bowed.

Her mother finally found her voice. "What about your plans for medical school?"

"Well, she can forget about that now," responded her father, angrily.

Crystal didn't know what to say, so she didn't say anything. Her mother urged her to speak, but she had no words.

"Crystal, how did you let this happen?" her mother sobbed.

"I'll tell you how. She's nothing but a whore," shouted her father.

The words hit Crystal hard, and she would have preferred if he had actually slapped her than call her a whore, especially in this case. Her mother tried to defend her and told her father not to say things like that, but he dismissed her pleas.

"I am a preacher. What will it look like for my own teenaged daughter to be with child? I will not allow you to bring a reproach on this family, and more importantly, my reputation as a man of God."

Although she would have been ashamed and

embarrassed to tell them about the rape, her father never even asked what happened, or really gave her space to explain. Her father strolled toward the front door without uttering another word.

"Henry!" her mother shouted his name.

He kept walking, and she called out to him again.

"Henry, what are we going to do about this?"

He spun around with the quickness, and with anger in his eyes and disgust in his voice, he replied, "We're not going to do anything. When I get home from church, I expect you to be gone." His remark was directed to Crystal.

"Gone? Where is she going to go, she's only a child."

"That's not my problem. She should have thought about that before she went out, acting like a whore and doing grown people things." He turned and strolled out of the house.

Crystal knew her mother loved her and wanted to help her, but her father was a tyrant, and whatever Henry said, Henry meant. Her mother had no choice. Crystal and her mother stood in the living room, hugging and sobbing. Henry shouted for her to come on, and her mother walked out the door, leaving a fifteen-year-old Crystal to figure out what her next move would be.

Crystal packed her things and left. Lisa's mother allowed her to stay at their house, but Crystal knew she couldn't stay there forever. Since Crystal didn't have the money to be treated by a physician, she continued to treat herself and the baby by reading books. She spent all her free time in the library. The reality of basically being homeless had her stressed out, and she couldn't get the rape out of her mind. She relived the incident every day.

The months flew by, and Crystal was eight months pregnant. Her mother knew she was staying at Lisa's, so she would check with Lisa's mother to make sure she was doing all right, but she was forbidden by Crystal's father to have anything to *do with Crystal. According to him, she had committed the ultimate sin, and this was the price she had to pay.*

One day, during her regular checks to see how Crystal was doing, it happened. Lisa's mother told her that Crystal's water had just broken, and they were on their way to the hospital.

Since this was Crystal's first baby, she was in labor for hours. When the baby finally arrived, Crystal was relieved and exhausted, but she got the surprise of her life. One baby came out, and then another. Crystal had identical twin girls. She didn't know what she would do now. This had just made things worse. It was going to be bad enough not having a place to live with one child; what was she going to do with two babies? When the nurses handed her the babies, she instantly fell in love all over again. Not having a home for them was the last thing on her mind at that time. She wanted to give her babies something that belonged to her. She decided their middle names would be her name.

Elissa Crystal and Jalissa Ann Johnson.

Crystal's parents were there for the birth. She was shocked her father had shown up, but he had. Her mother explained to her that her father had come to tell her she could come back home and finish high school, but after that, she had to leave home for good. Now that she'd had twins, things had changed. Henry commented that he refused to take care of three children, including Crystal in his count. He told Charlotte only one baby could stay with them, and the other had to live somewhere else. Charlotte inquired, through tears, where her other granddaughter would possibly go. Henry immediately used the phone in the hospital and called his brother and sister-in-law, Clifford and Bernice Johnson.

Bernice was unable to have children, so Henry swiftly arranged for them to take the other twin home with them, under one condition: they weren't allowed to bring the twin to family functions. Clifford and Bernice lived way out in Long Island,

NY, while Henry and Charlotte lived in Queens, so the odds of them running into each other were slim to none. Again, this was Henry's way of executing punishment on behalf of God for Crystal's sin of being a whore, as he put it. All this was done without Crystal's consent, and she cried uncontrollably, but she felt she didn't have a choice. At least now she and the babies would not be homeless.

Three days had passed, and Crystal's love for her babies grew. She loved them with a love she'd never felt before, or even knew existed, so choosing which one to give away was the hardest thing she'd ever had to do in her fifteen years of living. In her mind, she quickly made the decision to finish school, get her career going as a doctor, and retrieve her other daughter when the time was right. Her Uncle Clifford was no better than her father. He was just as mean, and he called himself a Christian, too, so she didn't want her daughter under his care longer than she needed to be.

Although she knew her family would make sure she never saw her other daughter again, her father agreed to let whichever daughter she gave away keep the name she'd given her. Today was the day, and Crystal was packed and ready to leave the hospital. She prayed to God to keep her daughter safe. Crystal held the twin she was giving away in her arms until her aunt and uncle arrived at the hospital. She wanted to remember everything about her; her scent, her face, just everything. Elissa had a birthmark on her right cheek. It was above her jawbone in the shape of a star that was darker than the rest of her skin color. My little star, Crystal thought and smiled. The star birthmark was implanted in Crystal's mind as her father took the baby from her arms and handed her to her Aunt Bernice.

Chapter Seven

Elissa felt maybe the Lord had been looking out for her after all. The day she decided to hire a private investigator, it was as if the information she needed dropped out of the sky. There was a bulletin board in the lobby of her building, which she rarely paid any attention to, but the royal blue business card being held to the board with a red thumbtack, caught her eye. Elissa felt impelled, and she called him and set up an appointment right away.

It was now a week later, and she had yet to hear back from him. His name was Chance. They'd already had a quick meeting at his office, and she had supplied him with all the information she'd obtained from Mrs. Green, Clifford, and Bernice. All she really needed was for him to get an address and she would handle the rest. If he weren't so handsome, she would have given him a hard time, but instead, she patiently waited for him to call her with whatever he might have found out.

Elissa couldn't remember the last time she had

gone out on a real date. Her entire life consisted of running and hiding, and that was a bad combination. She had always been consumed with resentment, hate and hurt, so she never really enjoyed life. Chance's presence alone made her realize that. Starting from the moment they met, and thereafter, whenever she thought about him, she found herself forgetting about her vendetta. She wasn't sure what it was about him. He proclaimed to be a Christian, so maybe that was what made her feel secure around him, and his milk chocolate complexion was a bonus.

She was in the middle of doing rounds at the hospital when her phone alerted her she had a message. If she was anything, she was a professional, so the vibration of her phone didn't affect her. She would check the message after she finished treating her patients. She completed Mr. Gilbert's chart and indicated she was prescribing him the medication, Plavix. She went to the private lounge room designated for the medical staff to check her message. Elissa reached inside the pocket of her lab coat and retrieved her phone.

Hi, Dr. Johnson… I'm calling to let you know I have some valuable information for you. Please call me at your earliest convenience… Chance.

She hastily called Chance back. She wasn't sure if she was excited to hear what he'd found out, or if she was just excited to hear his voice. She admitted to herself the latter was the true answer. She was more excited to hear Chance's voice, but she had to stick to the business at hand.

When Chance answered the phone, Elissa felt a flutter in her stomach. *So that's what butterflies feel like*, she thought. Chance spelled out the street name to where her grandparents lived in Bayside. Elissa entered the address into her cell phone. He confirmed her mother was married and was definitely estranged from her grandparents. He didn't find out any information about her father. Her mother's name was Crystal Johnson, and she had two grown children, a son and a daughter, but he found out something interesting about Crystal's other daughter.

Paging Dr. Elissa Johnson… Paging Dr. Elissa Johnson.

Elissa interrupted Chance and told him she was being paged and had to go. Chance tried to catch her before she hung up, but it was too late. He attempted to call her back several times but was unsuccessful. He left her a voicemail, requesting she call him back as soon as possible. He knew Elissa would go to her grandparent's home the first opportunity she got, but he wanted to prepare her for what lied ahead.

Later that evening, when Elissa got home, she checked her messages and noticed Chance had called her back several times. After checking the remainder of her messages, she made a mental note to return his call. The message from Ann came as a surprise. The two women hadn't spoken since Elissa had asked if she knew her grandparents. One of the messages was from Mrs. Green, which Elissa was anxious to hear. Mrs. Green thought Elissa would be interested in knowing Clifford had been shot but was doing okay. Mrs. Green hadn't mentioned anything about the house burning down, so that answered Elissa's question on if they were able to put the fire out without the house becoming a casualty. She wondered if Bernice had told Mrs. Green the true story about how Clifford had gotten shot. Little did she know, Mrs. Green felt Clifford had gotten exactly what he deserved, no matter who had shot him.

Elissa didn't feel like talking to anybody, so she made the decision to return calls later. Well, Chance was the exception. Maybe she'd call him before she went to bed tonight. She undressed and slipped into something more comfortable. She fired up her laptop and decided to compose a letter to her grandparents. She addressed it to her grandfather since it was his bright idea to give her away. She re-read the letter several times to make sure she hadn't left anything out. When she was pleased with its contents, she printed the letter and put it in an envelope. At first, she was going to mail it via United States Postal Service, but then she settled on delivering the letter herself and saving a stamp.

By the time she finished writing, proofing, and editing the letter, it was late. She debated on whether she should call Chance or wait until tomorrow. Her anxiety got the best of her, and she found herself dialing his number. A sleepy-sounding female answered the phone. Ms. Sleepy politely asked who was calling and Elissa informed her she had the wrong number and politely hung up. Elissa felt like a fool. What made her think a man as attractive as Chance was single? A black man with a job was bound to be taken, and Chance was no exception. Elissa conceded she'd gotten from Chance what she had hired him for, therefore, his required services were complete. She would be sure to put his check in the mail and keep it moving. Elissa really liked Chance, and hoped they could get to know each other on a more personal level after she settled all the chaos in her life, but disappointments and let-downs were the norm for her, so why should now be any different?

Elissa walked throughout her penthouse and turned out all the lights. She climbed into her king-sized bed that was laden with pillows, got comfortable, and clicked on the television. She reached and retrieved a prescription bottle from the nightstand. She rarely took the sleep aid because her life was just as bad asleep as it was awake, but she was disappointed about the situation with Chance and wanted to just sleep it off. She popped one of her prescribed sleeping pills and dozed off while watching reruns of the sitcom *Frasier*, and that was when the reoccurring nightmare began.

A fifteen-year-old Elissa was in church on a Sunday morning. The preacher was preaching, and the choir was singing. All of a sudden, all the attention was on her. Everyone in the church turned to her and started chanting and calling her a whore. Clifford kept saying she was a whore like her mother and wasn't going to amount to anything because whores were only good for one thing. The church rapidly spun around, and the figures appeared to be in 3D, but just like the last time, someone new was in the dream who hadn't been there before.

As of late, this new person in her dream had been nothing but a black, silhouette, but this time, the person appeared. In the corner, she spotted Ann silently crying while she was taunted by the others, but she didn't do anything to stop them. The room constantly spun, and Elissa felt as if she were falling into nothingness.

Elissa bolted up out of her sleep in a cold sweat, as always. The nightmare was nothing new, she'd had the same dream for years, but what threw her was Ann's presence. Elissa believed God used dreams to reveal things, so in her mind, Ann being in her dream was not just a coincidence, it meant something, and Elissa wanted to find out what.

It was 4:30 a.m., and she was wide awake and

couldn't fall back asleep. Her alarm was set to go off in an hour anyway, so she started preparing for work a little early. Elissa was sure to place the letter to her grandparents in her bag. If her schedule didn't get too hectic today and keep her at the hospital too late, she was going to deliver the letter when she got off.

She checked her messages during her lunch hour, and there was a call from Chance. She called him back and thanked him for his help, but said his services were no longer needed. She told him his check was in the mail. Elissa still didn't give him the opportunity to tell her what he'd found out about her mother's other daughter. It wasn't her intentions to be rude to him, she just wanted to cut all ties before she found herself more emotionally involved than she already was.

So far so good, it was already 3:30 p.m. and her day was still on schedule. She hadn't been paged for any emergency services, and so far, there weren't any unplanned patients added to her responsibilities for the day. Now all she had to do was make it to 5:00 p.m.

While en route to Bayside, the closer Elissa got, the more nervous she started to feel. It wasn't the same feeling she had when she went to Georgia to visit Clifford and Bernice. When it came to them, even though she had no love for them, she was familiar with who they were. Her grandparents were a different story. She didn't know these people at all. She wondered if she had any of their features or characteristics. *Snap out of it*, she said to herself. She had come to the conclusion they were no better than Clifford and Bernice, if not worse. It didn't matter what they looked like. They could look like twins for all she cared. The point was, they decided to give her away and for her to be treated maliciously just because her mother had her out of wedlock. So as far as Elissa was concerned, revenge was due to them also.

Chapter Eight

Bayside, Queens, wasn't as fancy and luxurious as Clifford and Bernice's neighborhood in Buckhead, Georgia, but Elissa found herself pulling up to another lovely home in a pleasant neighborhood. Elissa located the house number and sat in the car for a few minutes before getting out. She glanced around the neighborhood, taking in her surroundings. She realized the flag on the mailbox to her grandparents' home was raised, which was designed to signal that mail was in the box. This meant her grandparents hadn't yet checked their mail. She made the decision to place the letter in the mailbox. She didn't want to risk being seen because she really hadn't thought this out all the way through.

Elissa swiftly got out of the car and quickly placed the letter in the mailbox, and not a moment too soon. A few short minutes after she got back in the car, an older gentleman with salt and pepper hair, more salt than pepper, exited the house, walked to the end of the driveway, and retrieved the mail. Elissa was parked across the street and decided to stay and observe, just in case he opened the letter right there on the spot.

He flipped through the mail, and when he came upon the addressed letter, with no stamp on it, he looked up and down the street, but still paid no attention to Elissa's car. He opened the letter and started to read. His eyes widened, then his eyebrows connected with a frown. The concerned look on his face verified he was her grandfather. He continued to read, and the distress on his face grew. Her grandfather placed a hand over his heart and called for Charlotte to come quickly. Charlotte ran out of the house frantically, asking him what was wrong. He didn't speak, just handed her the letter with one hand and continued to rest the other hand over his heart.

A stunned Elissa watched everything from her vehicle. Again, she wanted them to pay, but she didn't want anyone to actually die. Despite that thought, however, she didn't budge to help him. Maybe deep down, she did want him to die. Her grandparents slowly stumbled back to the house, her grandfather holding onto her grandmother for support.

Elissa sat there a while longer and recollected the contents of the letter. She had basically told them she knew everything. She knew it was his decision for her to be given away to his brother and his wife. She revealed she knew it was his suggestion for her to be treated badly because of the sins of her mother. She expressed disdain for her grandmother for allowing it to happen. While writing that part of the letter, Elissa promised herself she would never become like her grandmother and great Aunt Bernice. Both of them were ruled and controlled by her grandfather and great uncle. In her eyes, they were poor excuses for women.

The letter was three pages long, but in a nutshell, she'd told them she was going to repay them for the terrible childhood she'd had. She didn't go into detail, just told them they didn't know where or when, but to always be on the lookout because they didn't know when she would strike. She casually mentioned that if they'd checked with Clifford and Bernice lately, they'd know she wasn't just making idle threats.

Elissa heard the sirens of an ambulance in the distance. The sirens were getting closer, and Elissa's gut feeling told her the ambulance was on its way to her grandparents' home. Elissa thought that was a good time to pull off. She got a few blocks down and had to pull over to give the ambulance space. It whizzed past her and stopped in front of her grandparents' home, just as she'd thought. She glanced in her rearview mirror and continued to drive. Her job was done here.

Elissa hadn't planned on stalking her grandparents. Who really had that kind of time? Her strategy was to disrupt their peace of mind and make them uncomfortable. She wanted them to be on pins and needles at all times, not knowing when she was going to make her move, when, in reality, *that* was her move. From the looks of things, as she thought back to her grandfather gripping his chest, her plan was already working like a charm. Now all she had to do was find out where her mother was, and her revenge would be complete.

She'd come too far to stop now. She considered calling Chance back and seeing if he could possibly locate her mother. Everyone said she was estranged from the family, and no one knew where she was, but she wasn't the invisible woman, so she had to be somewhere. It was just a matter of tenacity and perseverance.

She approached a red light, reached over to the passenger seat, and retrieved a piece of mail she'd removed from her grandparents' mailbox when she dropped off her letter. She didn't look at it when she removed it but figured it might be helpful, whatever it was. It was a reminder letter for a medical magazine subscription, addressed to

Crystal Johnson. She decided she wouldn't contact Chance, so she pondered on how that information could be helpful to her. She assured herself she would come up with something, and that was when the light bulb came on in her head. She'd already dealt with Clifford, Bernice, Henry, and Charlotte, now it was Crystal's turn. Elissa couldn't help but think, *Four down, and one to go*. She smiled at the thought.

* * *

During her drive home, Elissa couldn't help but wonder what condition her grandfather was in. Her gut instinct mixed with her medical expertise told her it probably wasn't all that serious; maybe just chest pains due to intense stress, which shouldn't cause much damage, if any at all. She couldn't linger on that thought. Bottom line, whatever happened to him would be what he deserved for the lifetime of discomfort he'd caused her, no matter how indirect it might have been.

She entered her penthouse, hung her keys on

the key rack in the kitchen, and removed her heels. Yes, heels. She walked the hospital floors all day, but she still had to remain classy, although she wasn't crazy enough to wear her five-inch heels.

She took a seat at the glass kitchen table and pulled out her phone and the piece of mail. Elissa sorted out in her head how the piece of mail addressed to her mother would be utilized. She crossed her fingers and hoped things would go the way she pictured it in her mind. She practiced changing her voice in order to sound like an older woman. She had a few tactics in mind. The one she would use depended on who answered the phone. When she figured she had it mastered, she dialed the 1-800 number listed on the subscription letter. After getting through the automated prompts by hitting zero on the dial pad for every option, she finally got a live person on the phone.

"Thank you for calling Medical Magazine. My name is Deonte'. How may I assist you today?" asked the customer service representative.

Deonte' came across as if he wanted the same thing she wanted in the relationship department. Elissa smirked at the vision of Deonte' she'd conceived in her mind. She envisioned Deonte' with arched eyebrows, his lips pursed as he spoke, putting extra emphasis on his T's and S's. She didn't have an approach for a gay guy, so she decided to go with the motherly tone.

"Hello, Deonte'. How are you doing today, young man?"

"I'm doing good, and yourself?"

"Same   here."

"So, how may I help you today?" Deonte' asked politely.

"My name is Crystal Johnson, and I just want to verify that you have my current address on file. I was sure I contacted your company, but I need to double check."

"Sure thing, ma'am, I can do that. May I have your account number?"

Elissa recited the account number from the

letter and waited as she heard Deonte' typing to get her information to come up.

"Yes, Ms. Johnson, you did call and update your file. I do see where we mailed something to an old address, but that has been corrected, and you will receive mail at the updated address." " OK, could you please give me the address you have on file, son, so I can be sure you have the correct information?"

Elissa knew that most likely, that wasn't company procedure, but she crossed her fingers and hoped Deonte' would give her the address and not request her to give it to him instead.

"Sure thing, Ms. Johnson."

That was music to Elissa's ears. She flipped the letter over and jotted down the address Deonte' gave her. She hung up with the representative, folded the letter, and stuck it into her purse.

Elissa had another sleepless night, overtaken

by the nightmare, but once again, the dream had another new detail. The other night, the appearance of Ann in the dream had thrown her for a loop. Tonight, the dream flowed as usual until the part where everyone was in her face, calling her a whore. She saw her own face was amongst the crowd. There was someone mixed in with the crowd who looked just like her. She bolted up in a cold sweat, as usual. Now, the question was, why was she calling herself a whore? Elissa came to the conclusion that once she completed getting vengeance, the nightmare would finally cease.

Chapter Nine

When Elissa arrived to work the following day, she trudged directly to her office on the top floor of the hospital. She put on her lab coat and locked her newly purchased purse in the bottom drawer of her desk. The receptionist had a message waiting for her from Dr. Harvey, the cardiologist who was scheduled to work the previous night. She handed Elissa a sticky note and a copy of a medical chart. The message indicated that Dr. Harvey had treated a patient last night in the emergency department, and the spouse of the patient requested her husband be treated by the best cardiologist on staff. Dr. Harvey was an excellent doctor, but it was no secret that Elissa was the best.

Dr. Harvey left the patient's room number and requested for Elissa to go over the chart and check in on the patient. Elissa tucked the chart under her arm and headed toward the elevators to the room Dr. Harvey had jotted down on the yellow sticky. Elissa didn't have any patients she had to check in on at that time, so she had a few moments to spare.

Elissa still hadn't read the medical chart. She was sure Dr. Harvey had made all the right decisions, she was only checking in on the patient to appease the family since they'd requested the best. When she entered the room, the older gentleman was asleep, and he was hooked up to a heart monitor. Elissa decided to glance at the file, just to see exactly what had happened to the patient. She opened the folder, and the papers slipped out of her hands. The name on the chart read Henry Johnson. It was her grandfather.

As she stooped down to gather the papers, she heard her grandfather make a grunting sound, then cough. She stood, and they stared at each other. Henry reached up and touched the right side of his face. He was trying to say something, but nothing was coming out. Elissa suddenly felt a surge of hate shoot through her like electricity. She felt hate like she'd never felt before. She looked into the eyes of the man who was responsible for her heartache.

She walked closer to him, and from the wide-eyed expression on his face, it was obvious he knew who she was. Elissa felt she was having an out-of-body experience. She knew she shouldn't do what she had in her mind, but she couldn't stop herself. She leaned over and whispered in her grandfather's ear.

"I hope you die and burn in hell," she said with intense hatred.

Henry began shaking in the hospital bed, and the heart monitor went haywire. He flailed his arms and reached for the call button. Elissa stood there, peering at him as she held the call button in her hand, and not once did she attempt to press the button.

"Now you know how it feels to reach out for help, only to find there's no hand there to help you," she spat through gritted teeth.

Elissa released the call button and let it fall to the floor, out of reach from Henry. She glared at him one last time and rushed out of the room before the nurses were alerted that he needed attention.

When Elissa reached the end of the hall, she took a glance backward and witnessed doctors and nurses rushing into Henry's room. Two doctors rushed past her, and one requested she follow them to the room to lend her expertise as they continued to walk swiftly in the direction of Henry's room. *If he dies, he dies*, thought Elissa. She told the doctors she would be there as soon as possible and proceeded to walk in the opposite direction with no intention of lending a helping hand.

Elissa never did check back to find out what her grandfather's outcome was. She'd planned on venturing out today and popping up at Crystal Johnson's address, so that was her only concern at the moment.

The day flew by, and Elissa couldn't get to her car fast enough. She reached into her purse to retrieve the letter that had her mother's address on it, but she couldn't find it. It must have fallen out of her purse when she put it in the drawer, but she didn't feel like going all the way back to the office to check. She couldn't remember the street address, but she remembered it was in Springfield Gardens. She figured she'd just make her way to Springfield Gardens and ask around, and with any luck, someone would point her in the right direction.

Elissa pulled up to the first corner store she spotted when she entered the Springfield Gardens area. The neighborhood was decent, so she felt safe parking her car and getting out. She planned to purchase some sort of snack and casually ask about Crystal Johnson, but to her surprise, things didn't work as anticipated, and she definitely wasn't prepared for what happened.

She entered the store, walked to the back, and grabbed a bag of Bonton cheese doodles from the rack, which was her favorite snack as a child, and a Crush orange soda out the fridge. The entire time she had an eerie feeling as if she was being watched. There was a man behind the deli counter, and another man working the cash register. The tension released when a young boy, who appeared to be about nine years old, ran in the store to purchase one of those small jugs of juice for a quarter. He rushed passed Elissa, dropped the quarter on the counter, and on the way out said, "Oh, hi, First Lady Jalissa."

Elissa remembered hearing that name before, but couldn't remember where. Then it hit her. The day she called Ann, her husband had called her Jalissa. She instantly had a feeling something was going on, but she didn't know what. Elissa placed her items on the counter and reached for her wallet. The man at the cash register, who resembled someone of Arabian descent, which was not uncommon in New York, peered at her questioningly.

"Mrs. Jalissa, are you feeling OK?" he asked in a heavy accent.

Elissa decided to play along because she knew she was on the brink of something.

"Yes, I'm fi-fine," she stammered.

"Okay, was just checking. Normally, you're

happy, smiling, talking about Jesus, but today, not so much."

"Thank you so much for your concern. I just have a headache, that's all," she smiled.

She opened her wallet to pay for her items, and Mr. Arabian reached out and put his hand over hers. Elissa jumped back in fear as if the man was trying to snatch her wallet.

"Mrs. Jalissa, you know your money isn't good here." He stared at her.

Elissa didn't know what to say, so she didn't say anything. She knew her reaction had startled him because when she jumped back, he removed his hand as if he'd touched something hot. She placed her wallet in her purse and waited for Mr. Arabian to put her items in a bag. He told her to hold on one minute because he had something for her. He spoke to the man behind the deli counter in their native tongue, then trotted to the back room. He returned with a big, brown cardboard box. Mr. Arabian explained he had a box of goodies for her that he was donating to the youth at her church. He carried the box to her car, complimented her new vehicle, suggested she get some rest, and told her to tell her husband, Reverend Hill, he said hello. Elissa wanted to get out of there as fast as possible. She thanked him and sped off like somebody was chasing her, all the while wondering who this *Jalissa* was. Elissa was sidetracked and decided to investigate this *Jalissa* situation. She would track Crystal down later.

Elissa didn't know why, but she had a sick feeling in her stomach. She had such a tight grip on the steering wheel, her knuckles had turned white. She drove for a few more blocks and decided to pull over to calm down. She felt lightheaded. *Maybe my sugar level is dropping*, she thought. Elissa reached in the back seat to open the box Mr. Arabian had given her to see if it contained something sweet. She noticed a bright pink sticky note on the side of the box.

Rev. Jason & Jalissa Hill – Pentecostal

Apostolic Church- Rochdale

Elissa grabbed a Little Debbie chocolate cupcake out of the box and retrieved her tablet that was in the passenger seat. She Googled the church name that was written on the sticky note, and an address immediately popped up. She wasn't far from Rochdale, so she decided to continue on this journey and see where it ended. She clicked 'get directions' on the webpage and let the prompts from the navigational program lead the way.

Pentecostal Apostolic Church was a large church near Rochdale Village that took up a great portion of the block. PASTOR JASON HILL & FIRST LADY JALISSA HILL were on the church marquee with a quote underneath that read, '70x7 (The Road to Forgiveness)'. The last thing Elissa wanted to think about was forgiveness, but the names on the church sign let her know she was in the right place, whatever that meant.

Elissa had no idea what she was going to do once she met this Jalissa, but for some reason, she felt there was a connection between the two of them. There were a group of neighborhood children hanging out in front of the church. Elissa came to the conclusion that the box from Mr. Arabian would come in handy for this situation. Elissa got out of her SUV and grabbed her purse and the box of goodies from the backseat.

"Hey, First Lady Hill," one of the young girls called out to Elissa.

"Do you need help with that box?" one of the young boys asked.

"I like your new truck," another child chimed in.

Elissa greeted the children with a smile, but she didn't want to actually *say* much, so she gave the children one-word answers. Elissa concluded now was as good a time as any to distract the children, who appeared to be in the age range of nine through eleven, with the snack box.

When Elissa broke open the box with cakes, cookies, chips and candy bars, it seemed the

103

number of children multiplied like gremlins. Children came from everywhere to get dibs on the snacks. Elissa left the box of goodies on the church steps for the children to enjoy. She assumed with a church this size, someone had to be at the church, so she pulled on the church door, and it opened. Elissa heard singing coming from the sanctuary. She peeped in and witnessed a group of older ladies sitting in the choir stand. *Must be the missionary choir*, she assumed. Elissa didn't know what she was looking for, but she crept through the church, silently praying she didn't run into anyone. She glided down the long church hallway until she came upon an office door with a gold nameplate that read First Lady Jalissa Hill. *BINGO!!*

Elissa twisted the knob, and the door was unlocked. She didn't want to linger too long and end up getting busted, so she quickly rifled through the desk, searching for anything that may have appeared to be important. She found a calendar in the right upper hand drawer. She quickly opened the calendar and took a picture with her cell phone of the page of the current month and the following month. She turned to the *Note* page in the calendar and took a picture of that page also. Elissa continued to search the desk drawers. She came across a Rolodex in the bottom drawer. Quickly flipping through the small index cards, she realized it was loaded with phone numbers, addresses, and other information. Elissa figured this one wouldn't be missed, since there was a nicer one on the desk, so she put the old Rolodex in her purse and eased out of the office.

She'd almost made it out of the church undetected, but that was too good to be true. As she crept back down the long hallway, toward the front door, one of the ladies came out of the sanctuary.

"Praise the Lord, First Lady Hill," greeted the lady to Elissa's back.

Elissa kept walking and ignored the lady. The lady called out to Elissa again, and again, Elissa ignored her. The lady pursued her, calling out and asking her what was wrong. Elissa picked up her pace and started to jog down the hall the rest of the way to the door. She made it to the front door, snatched it open, trotting to her vehicle, and drove off without looking back. Things were starting to get weird with this Jalissa issue. It had been said everyone has a twin, and clearly, Jalissa must be hers, but she still felt the urge to find out more about First Lady Jalissa Hill. Elissa couldn't shake the feeling that this situation ran deeper than the cliché *everyone had a twin*.

This whole thing was getting more bizarre by the minute. She wanted to talk to someone, and Ann came to mind. She would have gone to Ann's home, but it dawned on her she didn't know where she lived and she hadn't spoken to her in a few days, either. Elissa decided to go home.

Chapter Ten

Elissa was greeted by Mr. Bradley, the doorman. He told her she'd had a visitor earlier from a young man who appeared to be in his early twenties. Chance was the first one to come to mind, but he wasn't in his twenties, so Elissa dismissed that thought. Mr. Bradley had started working in her building a little over five years ago. Word was, he owned the company that employed doormen for luxury apartments in Manhattan. He had decided to work in her particular building to remain in the swing of things.

Mr. Bradley was always the perfect gentleman. He'd never disrespected Elissa. Although he was old enough to be her father, for some men, that wouldn't have made a difference. Contrary to him being the father figure he exemplified, there were a few times when she caught him staring at her, but it wasn't with a lustful look. At those times, she couldn't put her finger on it, but there was a dark look in his eyes. The glare was always fleeting, and he would switch up before he thought she'd noticed.

When he informed Elissa she'd had a visitor

earlier, she was assured he'd thoroughly screened the individual. Mr. Bradley handed her a manila envelope left by the visitor. Elissa thanked Mr. Bradley and went to the mailbox to retrieve her mail. She flipped through her mail as she waited for the elevator. Black credit card bill, Nordstrom's department store bill, and last, but definitely not least, student loan bill. She felt like breaking out in song and singing "Bills, Bills, Bills" by Destiny's Child. The next piece of mail she came across wasn't a bill, and instead of her hands flipping through the mail, her stomach was doing the flips. Elissa stepped onto the elevator with the manila envelope tucked under her arm, and an unexpected letter in her hand.

Elissa stepped inside her space, anxious to see the contents of both envelopes. The package from the visitor was still a mystery, but the letter she held in her hands was from Chance. He had been calling, but Elissa had ignored him. She really wanted to return his calls, but judging from the sound of the woman who answered his phone when she last called him, she thought better of it, so she didn't call him back.

She sat on the couch, kicked her shoes off, and leaned back against the plush pillows. She tucked one leg under the other and opened the letter. To her surprise, it wasn't an actual letter, but a greeting card. It was a Mahogany friendship card with black silhouettes of a male and female facing each other, shaking hands. They were introducing themselves, but cupid was in the upper corner of the card, preparing to shoot his love arrow. The pre-printed words expressed there's nothing like a genuine friendship, and how good friends are hard to find. Chance had written a personal note inside the card, which read, *This card speaks the sentiments of my heart. I know we haven't known each other long, but I would like to change that. Let's start with dinner. Let me know.*

There was also a separate piece of paper inside the card, which changed the whole mood of the moment. The note requested that she please give him a call because he had some information he was sure she would be interested in. Elissa decided she would call him back after she reviewed the contents in the other envelope. She didn't know what she was about to encounter, but her gut told her she was about to experience the shock of her life.

Elissa went to the kitchen to pour herself a glass of white wine, just in case she needed something to calm her nerves. She slowly opened the envelope as if she worked on the bomb squad and was deactivating a bomb with only minutes to spare. The envelope contained pictures and a note.

I know it's probably too late for us, and that breaks my heart more than you'll ever know, but I thought it was time you knew the truth. Love your mother!

Elissa's hands shook uncontrollably as she re-read the note. The obvious questions immediately popped into her head. Was this package *really* from her mother? If so, how did her mother know where she lived? And who had dropped off the package?

Elissa flipped through the pictures frantically. Photo after photo, she looked at pictures that contained her face, the only problem was, it wasn't her in the photos. She had never seen the people in the pictures before in her life, but the woman in the photo was the spitting image of her. There were photos of the woman with a handsome man, which probably was her husband, and there were photos of the woman with two beautiful, identical young girls, who were probably her twin daughters. There was a photo of the woman who appeared really classy and first lady-like with a church hat, shoes, and purse to match.

The woman in the pictures was happy, which was another indication that it wasn't her. The woman looked just like her physically, but the smile on the woman's face was one Elissa had never seen on her own face. She felt like she was in a trance looking at the photos. Her cell phone rang, and her trance was broken. It was Chance, and whereby she would usually ignore his calls, she was going to call him tonight anyway, so she went ahead and answered. She prayed he wouldn't hear the shakiness in her voice.

"Hello."

"Well, hello, stranger. I'm so glad you answered the phone."

"I'm sorry. My apologies, I've just been so busy," she lied.

"Did you get my card?" Elissa could tell Chance was smiling.

"Yes, I got it today. Thanks so much. That was sweet of you." Now she was also smiling.

"Hopefully, you'll take me up on my offer one day."

"Maybe I will," Elissa replied.

There was a brief moment of silence, and Chance spoke again.

"This is also a business call."

"Yes, I was going to call you tonight. What is this information you have for me?"

"It's about the investigation I was doing for you. It's about your mother's other daughter."

Elissa had a feeling she already knew what he was going to say, but she needed to actually hear it.

"What about her?" Elissa asked hesitantly.

"Elissa, you are a twin. You and your sister are identical. Your mother kept your sister and raised her. I'm not sure where your mother is today, she's a little harder to track down, but I confirmed this information, and you are definitely a twin."

Elissa really didn't need convincing; she knew in her heart it was true. Elissa had a follow-up question on the tip of her tongue, and although she knew the answer, again, she needed to actually hear it.

"What is my sister's name?"

"Her name is Jalissa Ann Hill. She's married to a preacher. They live in your mother's old house in Springfield Gardens. Your mother moved and gave the house to your sister."

"Sounds like Jalissa got the better end of the

deal," she mumbled under her breath.

"What was that?" Chance asked.

"Oh, nothing, I'm just shocked by this information."

"I know this is probably a lot to take in, so I'll leave you to your thoughts. You've already paid me for my services, so I know my job is done here, but if you ever need a friend to talk to, you have my number," Chance offered.

"I hate to be rude and rush you off the phone, but yes, this is a lot for me to process right now. Can I call you in a few days?"

"Sure you can. I'll be waiting," Chance remarked genuinely.

After hanging up with Chance, Elissa grabbed the photos again and peered at them with newfound hatred. She hated her sister for being the one her mother had decided to love. Why wasn't she chosen to be loved? Elissa thought about the Bible story of Esau and Jacob. To make a long story short, Jacob was loved by Rebekah, their mother, and Esau wasn't. Jacob got the blessing and Esau didn't. She compared that to the story of her life. Esau and Jacob — Elissa and Jalissa. In the Bible story, Esau vowed to kill Jacob for taking his blessing. Elissa hadn't planned on actually taking Jalissa's life, but when she was through, Jalissa would wish she were dead.

Since her mother had done a disappearing act and wasn't easy to find, getting revenge on Jalissa would serve a dual purpose. For one, she would make sure Jalissa knew what it felt like to encounter hardship in life, and in doing so, she was sure this would pull her incognito mother out of hiding. It was clear Jalissa was her favorite, so when she learned that her *favorite* was suffering, Elissa was sure she would make an appearance.

Chapter Eleven

The next day, Elissa definitely wasn't in the mood to go to work. For one, she had a slight hangover from the wine she had drunk last night. It started out as one glass, and then quickly turned to half of the bottle. Elissa rested in the bed a few more hours before getting up and starting her day. She decided to utilize more of the many hours of vacation time she had accumulated. She'd just returned from Georgia, but Elissa was a workaholic, and never really took time off.

When the clock struck 11:00 a.m., she got up to brew a cup of coffee in her Keurig coffee maker. She moved about her apartment in slow motion. She strolled to the bathroom to turn on the shower. She caught a glimpse of her reflection in the bathroom mirror and stopped and stared at her oval face, arched eyebrows, slightly plumped lips, butterscotch complexion, jet-black hair with a short Halle Berry haircut, and a star-shaped birthmark that was darker than her skin color on the right side of her face, above her jawbone. She didn't know why, but she hated her birthmark. She thought it was odd looking, and she always made sure it was covered up with concealer. She rarely went out in public without it being covered if she could help it. Only a few people knew it was there. She continued to stare in the mirror, and it was eerie that someone else had the same exact face as her. It was also eerie that she and Jalissa had the same haircut. Maybe it was true what they said about the connection twins had with one another. Elissa slightly touched her birthmark and wondered if her twin had one also.

After Elissa showered and dressed, she remembered the Rolodex in her purse and the pictures she had taken of Jalissa's calendar. She now had access to the church's schedule as well as Jalissa's personal schedule for the next two months. The Rolodex contained numbers for everything. From her children's school to the head bishop of their church's organization, and that was when the thought hit her.

Elissa jumped up, grabbed her keys, and exited her penthouse. She sped walked to the storage area where each tenant had a personal storage unit. She unlocked her unit and went inside. It took her no time to find what she was looking for. She retrieved a decorative animal print box from the bottom shelf and trotted back to her apartment. Back inside, she carefully selected the pictures she needed for her special assignment.

Elissa went through the Rolodex and the calendar again with a fine-toothed comb. She entered numbers in her cell phone she thought were important and entered certain events on her own calendar from Jalissa's calendar. She now also had Jalissa's and Jason's cell numbers. From the note section of Jalissa's calendar, there was a four-digit passcode written on a blue sticky. Elissa hoped it went to something important. Elissa would check later to see if the passcode went to Jalissa's or Jason's cell phone. She would check that out later, but right now, she had something else she wanted to do.

Elissa grabbed her cell phone, pressed *67 to block her number, and dialed.

"Praise the Lord, this is First Lady Jalissa speaking," Jalissa answered cheerily.

"I'm going to ruin your life."

The cheerful tone in Jalissa's voice immediately departed.

"Excuse me?"

"You heard me. I'm going to ruin your life."

"I'm sorry, you must have the wrong number."

"You wish I had the wrong number, Jalissa."

"Who is this? How did you get my number?" Jalissa asked fearfully.

"You'll find out soon enough who I am, but for now, I have a riddle for you. When you look at yourself, you're also looking at me."

Elissa pressed the 'End Call' button on her cell phone. After the phone call to Jalissa, Elissa dressed, and walked to the nearest Walgreens, then to the post office. The sun was shining, and the temperature was perfect. It was about seventy degrees, and Manhattan was lively. Elissa needed to do some research, so she went back home and completed her research on the roof of the penthouse, by the pool, while enjoying the sun.

Her research session didn't take long at all. She needed to find out if there was a community paper, newsletter, or something of that nature for the Springfield Gardens and/or Rochdale area. Elissa did a Google search and eventually learned that both areas had a community newsletter, and today was the deadline for submissions. If she delivered information to both papers today, her articles would be printed in the next edition, which went out every Monday. Elissa contacted both offices to let them know she had an article she thought they'd be interested in. The receptionist from both places advised her to get the articles turned in before 5:00 p.m. if she wanted them to be considered for print in the next release.

After Elissa dropped off the articles at both places, with only minutes to spare, she started feeling antsy. She couldn't just sit around, waiting for Monday to come. She pondered on ways to keep busy since it was indefinite when she was going to return to work; it all depended on how fast things progressed. Elissa still upheld her professional work ethics, so she informed the hospital she would be on call and could be contacted in case of emergencies, but she wouldn't be coming in every day.

According to the calendar, Jalissa and Jason were at the church every day, except when either had outside appointments or things to do for their daughters. It was clear their positions at the church were their actual jobs. Jason was the senior pastor, and Mrs. 'I'm so perfect, with my perfect family, and perfect life', First Lady Jalissa, was the church's administrator.

Elissa intended to ride by the church after she finished delivering the articles, but it was getting late, so she drove home and planned to return to Queens the next day. It was a hike driving from her penthouse in Manhattan to Queens, and not to mention, the high price of gas. Elissa came to the conclusion she would rent a room at a nearby hotel in Queens.

The next morning, Elissa packed an overnight bag. She stopped by the hospital to get a few things she needed and headed toward Queens. She checked in at the Crowne Plaza near JFK Airport. Elissa dropped her overnight bag off in the room and headed to Rochdale. It was 9:00 a.m. and Jalissa was scheduled to be at the church at 9:30 a.m. Elissa intended to arrive at the church before Jalissa. She parked down the street and waited for Jalissa to show up. Jason was scheduled for a breakfast meeting with some of the local pastors, which meant he wouldn't be at the church this morning.

Jalissa pulled up and parked in her designated spot labeled *First Lady Hill*, in the parking lot in back of the church. Elissa waited for Jalissa to enter the church, then she pulled her truck up next to Jalissa's car. They even had the same brand vehicle, except Elissa's was an SUV, and Jalissa had a sedan. Elissa retrieved the needed items from under her seat and got out of the truck. She entered the church using the same door Jalissa used minutes before. It was quiet inside, and the other associates who worked at the church had not yet arrived. Jalissa was the only one there.

Elissa eased down the hallway. She knew where Jalissa's office was from the other day, and since she had come through the back door, she didn't have to walk down the long hallway to get there. Jalissa was playing a Fred Hammond CD and checking her emails with her back to the door. She never heard Elissa coming. Elissa slipped in the office behind Jalissa and covered her mouth with a towel doused with chloroform. In a matter of minutes, Jalissa had slumped over and was out cold. Elissa grabbed Jalissa's purse, and it was a bit of a struggle, but she finally got Jalissa to her truck. She forced her in the backseat and left the chloroform towel over her face to guarantee she wouldn't wake up before Elissa wanted her to. Elissa removed Jalissa's cellphone from her purse. She studied a few texts between Jalissa and Jason, just to get an idea of how they communicated with each other. She didn't want anything to appear suspicious just yet.

Hey hubby, I forgot about the all-day women's seminar at Holy Ghost Fire Church of God in Staten Island. Sister Jackson was waiting at the church for me... I rode with her. My car is at the church. JH

OK honey, no problem. Will you be finished in time to meet me for our date night tonight? Pastor Hill

Sure hubby ☺ JH

I'll see you at 8:00 p.m. Love you. Pastor Hill

Make it 9:00 p.m. just to be sure. Love you too. JH

Elissa wanted everything to appear as normal, so she didn't ask Jason where they were meeting for date night. She prayed the information would be in Jalissa's phone. She opened the calendar on Jalissa's cell phone, and there it was. The girls were spending the night with Jalissa's mother, and tonight, the date night was in-house. Elissa decided to have some fun with her new brother-in-law to pass the time.

Elissa arrived back at the hotel with an incoherent Jalissa. She solicited the assistance of the concierge. She informed him her twin sister was just released from the hospital and was very weak. Elissa had put a hospital band on Jalissa's arm and everything to make it look legit. Elissa also revealed she was a doctor and the concierge was more than willing to lend a helping hand. He helped Elissa get Jalissa to her suite.

A few hours later, and Jalissa finally came to. She slightly struggled, but quickly realized she was tied to a chair with duct tape around her mouth.

Jalissa was still groggy and tried to scream, but nothing came out. Her vision was blurry, but she was able to make out a woman sitting across from her on the king-sized bed, doing something on a laptop. Jalissa tried to figure out where she was, but the last thing she remembered was sitting in her office at the church, but this wasn't her office, and she wasn't at the church.

She attempted to scream again, but between the duct tape and her state of confusion, the attempt was once again futile.

Elissa glanced over and realized Jalissa was awake. She rose from the bed and approached Jalissa. Elissa ripped the duct tape from her mouth, and Jalissa let out a slight moan. Elissa sat back down on the bed and stared at Jalissa. *Amazing*, she thought. Same oval face, arched eyebrows, slightly plumped lips, butterscotch complexion, jet-black hair, and a short Halle Berry haircut. It was uncanny how much they resembled. It was literally like looking in the mirror.

"So you're the one that's been popping up in my dreams lately," whispered Elissa.

Jalissa's vision was still blurred, which hindered her from realizing that the woman who held her hostage, shared her face. Jalissa lazily lifted her head to look at Elissa, but her head was too heavy. She let her head fall back and rock from side to side.

"Who are you?" whispered a scared Jalissa.

"Well, isn't it obvious? I'm you. Well, at least I'll be you until my mission is accomplished. "

"What do you mean?"

"You'll find out soon enough."

"Who are you?" Jalissa inquired again.

"Are you blind? Look at me. We're twins!!"

"Twins?"

"Now, you're deaf, too? Yeah, twins."

"What do you mean?"

"Now, you're also dumb? Maybe we're *not* twins," stated Elissa sarcastically.

"You're mistaken. I don't have a twin sister."

"Well, we learn something new every day, hunh? Let me break it down for you. Your mother, I mean, *our* mother, gave birth to twins. She gave me away to be abused and treated like garbage, while she kept you and treated you like a princess."

Another Bible story came to Elissa's remembrance, just as the story of Esau and Jacob had done earlier. Hearing Jalissa express she didn't have a twin sister made Elissa feel that much more rejected by her mother. Elissa concluded her biological mother had accepted Jalissa but didn't even want to give Elissa a chance. How did her mother know she wouldn't have fulfilled her and offered her happiness just by being her daughter? Instead, she'd been rejected prematurely.

Cain and Abel, she thought. In the Bible, Abel's offering was accepted by the Lord, and Cain's offering was rejected. Cain became upset and wanted to make his brother pay for being *accepted,* so Cain murdered him. Of course, in this scenario, she was Cain. For the first time, she despised her name. Elissa Crystal, initials EC. E for Esau, and C for Cain. Then she compared her sister's name, Jalissa Ann, initials JA. J for Jacob, and A for Abel.

I must have been destined for destruction and rejection, thought Elissa. Elissa peered at Jalissa with contempt and reckoned that getting revenge on her was going to be so sweet — sweet like Cain, and she didn't mean sugar cane.

Jalissa was still disoriented from the chloroform, but she found enough strength to plead with Elissa to let her go. She repeatedly told Elissa she must have the wrong person because she didn't have a twin. Elissa ignored her, checked her watch, and realized the hour was getting late, and she had to get ready. Elissa warned Jalissa against attempting to draw attention to the room. She told her she knew where she lived, and she was sure Jalissa wouldn't want any harm to come to that perfect little family of hers.

"But my husband will start to worry and look

for me if I'm not home by a certain time," Jalissa tried to reason. "Let me go, and I won't say anything." Now, she was crying.

"Oh, don't worry about your husband, I got that covered."

Elissa undressed, removed Jalissa's clothing, and put them on. She untied Jalissa from the chair but left her hands bound. She ordered for a still disoriented Jalissa to get on the bed. Elissa extended one last warning to Jalissa about trying to escape, but just to be on the safe side, she placed the chloroform towel back over her nose and duct taped her hands to the bedpost.

Elissa felt she still needed additional reinforcement, so she reached inside her purse and removed a few items she'd *borrowed* from the hospital. She ripped open the plastic and removed the content: a 12ml syringe. Elissa stuck the tip of the needle into the small glass bottle and pulled the plunger down as she watched the morphine fill the barrel of the syringe. Elissa prepped Jalissa's arm and waited for a vein to pop up. She inserted the needle into Jalissa's arm and pushed the plunger, releasing the morphine into Jalissa's vein. It was the smallest dosage possible so it wouldn't kill her, but it would knock her out really well, and let her get the best sleep she'd probably ever had. When Elissa was confident that she one hundred and twenty percent looked like Jalissa, she strolled out of the hotel room.

It was already 9:00 p.m., so Elissa used Jalissa's phone to text Jason.

Hubby, I'm on my way home, got something special in mind. We can skip right to dessert, if you know what I mean ☺ JH

Wow! Who is this and what did you do with my wife? Pastor Hill

Elissa immediately became worried. Did he know what was going on?

What do you mean by that?

Nothing honey, you're just never this forward, but I like it ☺ Pastor Hill

Elissa relaxed.

Well I figured it was time you saw my dark side.
xoxo JH

I can't wait. I'll be upstairs waiting for you.
Hurry up. Pastor Hill

Chapter Twelve

Your destination is on the right, announced the voice from the GPS. The house was beautiful. Elissa looked up at the house while still inside her truck and noticed all the lights were out, except for a lit room on the second floor. This let Elissa know where the master bedroom was. She prayed Jason was upstairs because she didn't want him to realize that she wasn't who she was portraying to be just yet. It took her three attempts to find the key to the house from Jalissa's key ring. She tried to ease in the house quietly, but Jason heard her come in.

"Hurry up, honey," Jason yelled from upstairs.

"Okay," Elissa responded with a one-word answer.

She didn't want her voice to give her away, although she and Jalissa did sound alike.

"Be up in a minute," she added.

Elissa located the kitchen and poured two glasses of red wine that she had purchased from the store. She knew the good ole Reverend, and straitlaced Jalissa probably didn't have any alcohol in the house. She reached in her purse, or better yet, 'bag of tricks', and fumbled around until she found her pill case. Earlier, Elissa had crushed three of her sleeping pills to a fine powder. She opened the cap and let the powder fall into the glass of wine intended for Jason. With both glasses of wine in hand, and her purse hanging from her shoulder, Elissa proceeded upstairs. The bedroom door was closed, and the light emitted from under the door.

"Baby, my hands are full," she said through the door. "Could you open the door for me? But first, I need you to turn out the lights."

Elissa heard the click of the light switch and the room went black. Jason opened the door with nothing but his boxers on. The only light in the room was from the street lights outside, just the way Elissa wanted it.

At first, Elissa was doing this out of spite, but she took one look at Jason and resolved that pictures did him no justice. He put her in the mind of Blair Underwood, just a few shades darker. He was very attractive, and she was going to enjoy this. She handed him his glass of wine. The good ole reverend rejected the wine at first, replying she knew he didn't indulge, and it was to his knowledge, she didn't, either. Elissa tried to lighten the mood by joking that even the disciples drank wine. Jason smiled and shook his head while accepting his glass from her hands and agreed this was a one-time thing. Elissa agreed this would be the first and last time.

Elissa set her glass of wine down on the dresser and pranced into the adjacent bathroom to freshen up. When she emerged from the bathroom, all she had on was her black lace undergarments. She peered at the nightstand and realized Jason's glass was empty. *Just a matter of time*, she thought.

Jason was in bed, waiting for her. She straddled him and blindfolded him with a silk scarf. Once again, Jason was caught off guard. This was not the Jalissa he knew, but he felt so relaxed, he just went

135

with it. Elissa leaned down and kissed Jason, and he kissed her back. Sleeping with her sister's husband was not the ultimate revenge she had in mind for Jalissa, but this was going to be a bonus, and oh how sweet it would be.

She planned to go all the way until a Bible verse popped into her head. Talk about awkward. Now was not the time for Bible verses. She tried to continue because Jason was really getting involved, and she liked it, but the Bible verse wouldn't go away. Elissa didn't even know where the verse was found, nor could she remember exactly how it was worded. It was a verse she recalled hearing when she was a teenager. She vaguely remembered it being in the book of Romans. It said something about avenge not yourself because vengeance belonged to the Lord. The verse plagued her, and she couldn't continue no matter how much she really wanted to. Jason picked up on her hesitancy and questioned what was wrong.

Elissa aggressively removed the blindfold. Jason adjusted his eyes to the darkness and posed the question again. Elissa was frustrated because, once again, Jalissa was winning.

"How does it feel to almost cheat on your wife?"

"Honey, what are you talking about?"

"I'm not your honey," Elissa remarked angrily.

"OK, babe, this role-playing is going too far," Jason whispered sleepily.

The sleep aid Elissa had slipped into Jason's drink was taking effect, but she wanted him alert enough to know what was going on. She slapped him across the face in order to make him more attentive.

"Look at me," she hissed.

Still straddling him, Elissa reached over and turned on the lamp on the nightstand. She leaned in once again and stared at Jason. They were touching, nose to nose. There were a few moments of silence which felt like forever. Jason stared back at Elissa as if he was looking right through her, and when his eyes widened, that let her know he knew something was off. Jason jumped, and Elissa almost fell off of him and onto the floor.

"Who are you," he yelled, "and what did you do with my wife?"

Although Jason was too weak to do any real harm to Elissa, she still didn't want to take any chances. She got off of Jason and reached into her bag of tricks again and came out with her .22 caliber handgun. She aimed it at him and noticed the fear in his eyes as he slowly sat up in the bed. Jason had no idea what was going on. Elissa explained to him that she was Jalissa's long-lost twin sister. Jason questioned where Jalissa was, and Elissa told him she was with her, and they were using this little reunion to get to know each other better. Jason questioned Jalissa's safety, and Elissa continued to explain Jalissa was safe, for now.

Elissa expressed to Jason if he wanted Jalissa to remain unharmed, he would do exactly what she told him. She told him not to tell anyone, and definitely don't call the cops if he wanted to see Jalissa alive again. Jason shook his head in cooperation. Elissa told him he would be getting a text with further instructions.

The Lunesta was doing its job. That particular sleep aid was designed to cause relaxation and help one fall asleep and stay asleep. Jason asked her why she was doing this, but before she even had time to answer the question, Jason's head fell back into the pillows, and he was out. Elissa dressed and left. She sat in her truck for a few minutes before driving off. Sleeping with her sister's husband was pushing it, and she just couldn't bring herself to do it, but getting revenge was still a go. Jalissa wasn't going to get off that easily.

The weekend flew by so quickly, and before Elissa knew it, it was Monday morning. The day she was waiting for. She had barely gotten any sleep the night before. She'd kept Jalissa sedated with morphine and the sleep aid for the entire weekend. Elissa wasn't completely bad; she did at least try to feed Jalissa, but she really didn't have an appetite. Jalissa continued to weakly plead her case, saying Elissa was making a big mistake because her mother had never mentioned she had a twin. Elissa communicated with Jason via text and made sure he kept silent if he wanted his precious Jalissa to remain alive. Elissa hadn't planned on committing a homicide, but planting that seed in Jason's head kept him in line. She reiterated to him to not do anything other than what she ordered him to do and when she ordered him to do it. He reluctantly agreed.

Elissa made sure Jalissa was knocked out before she left the hotel. She drove to both neighborhoods to retrieve the newsletters. It was still very early in the morning, but Elissa wanted to make sure she got her copies before they were all gone.

PROMINENT FIRST LADY'S PAST COMES BACK TO HAUNT HER. WHAT'S

DONE IN THE DARK, WILL COME TO THE LIGHT!!

That was the headline for the community paper for Springfield Gardens. There were also a few pictures of First Lady Jalissa, cuddled up with various young men. Each picture was with a different man, and the photos suggested they were more than friends. The photos were old, but it was still around the time she was married to the ever so faithful and loyal Pastor Jason Hill.

IT'S TRUE WHAT THEY SAY, YOU CAN'T JUDGE A BOOK BY ITS COVER!!

That was the headline for the Rochdale community paper. This article included side by side photos of Jalissa. One was a picture of her decked out in her Sunday's best with hat, shoes, and purse to match. The other photo was a picture of Jalissa, relaxing in a hot tub with a man who wasn't her husband. The photos in both papers were clear shots of Jalissa, which left no room for denial. To make a long story short, both articles pretty much stated Mrs. First Lady Jalissa was not the holy, sanctified lady she claimed to be, or worse, not the woman the community and church thought she was. They pretty much called her a phony and a hypocrite and moved on to the next story of the week.

When Elissa got back to the hotel, Jalissa was awake, although barely. Her vision was still blurry, so she still hadn't realized she and her abductor shared the same facial features, but that was about it. Elissa was waiting for one last piece of her revenge puzzle, and everything would fall into place as she'd planned. With that thought in mind, she flipped open her laptop and checked her email account.

Jalissa had fallen asleep again, and Elissa looked over at her from the desk she was sitting at and felt a twinge of regret. As a child, she was forced to attend church, and because of that, and the fact her aunt and uncle claimed to be Christians but didn't act like it, she swore when she was grown, she was not going to attend church. But, some of the sermons she'd heard as a child seemed to pop into her head at the oddest of times, now being one of those times.

She recalled a message about love and forgiveness. The preacher explained God was love and that forgiveness was necessary, even if the other person was at fault. She'd always wanted a sister, and a twin would have been a bonus. Jalissa stirred in the bed, and Elissa was brought back to reality. She looked away from Jalissa and logged into her Gmail account. Things had gone too far anyway. Even if she'd wanted to change her mind, it was too late to turn back now.

Elissa scrolled through her emails until she came across the one she'd been waiting for. Last week, she'd mailed a letter, along with some photos, to the head bishop of Jalissa's church organization. She requested the bishop or someone from his office to contact her once the package was received. She'd enclosed her phone number and email address. She clicked on the email, and it opened.

Greetings, Ms. Johnson,

I'm sending this message to let you know I've received your package, and let me begin by saying, it was very disturbing, and I speak for the entire staff of ministers, bishops, and the entire Pentecostal Apostolic Church Organization when I say this type of behavior will not be tolerated. Pastor Jason and First Lady Jalissa came highly recommended, but it's clear that Satan will use anyone.

The photos of First Lady Jalissa were upsetting and unacceptable. I understand that being a member of this prestigious church, you were also disturbed when you happened upon the photos of First Lady Hill. Rest assured an emergency, impromptu meeting has been scheduled. I'm not at liberty to divulge all the details of the meeting, but you can take comfort in knowing that God is not pleased with this type of behavior, and neither is the organization. I pray you don't let this incident cause you to change your membership.

God bless you, sister.

Bishop Martin

Elissa logged out of her email account and turned off the laptop. Bishop Martin hadn't given the needed details about the meeting, and that put Elissa at a disadvantage until she remembered. She got Jalissa's cellphone and called the voicemail, and when prompted to enter the passcode, Elissa entered the four digit number she'd found in Jalissa's calendar, but the code did not work.

"Think, Elissa, that code has to go to something," she said out loud.

Elissa dialed the church's number, and it went straight to voicemail. Elissa bypassed the options of leaving a message and entered the prompts to access the messages. She entered the passcode and crossed her fingers. The code worked, and she retrieved the message from Bishop Martin, indicating the meeting would be held tonight at the church at 6:00 p.m. Elissa called Jason and told him she knew about tonight's meeting, and she demanded that he be there. She made it clear that if he tried anything funny, she couldn't promise the safe return of his beloved Jalissa. She informed him all he had to do was show up, and she would do all the talking. He was instructed to nod and point like a good little Pinocchio. In other words, she made it clear she was the one pulling the strings, and his job was to agree with everything she said.

Jason felt sick to his stomach, but he didn't have a choice but to go along with his sister-in-law's plan. He agreed with her demands with hopes that this whole nightmare would be over soon if he cooperated. Jason thought about calling his mother-in-law in order to straighten this whole thing out, but then he thought better of it. What was the use? He'd looked in the face of the stranger, and she was definitely the spitting image of his wife, Jalissa. They were incontestably twins.

Elissa had gone shopping earlier to find an outfit that was Jalissa's style. She came across the perfect black and white first lady suit in Sasha's in Green Acres Mall, along with black and white accessories, and as always, shoes and bag to match.

The day had gone by so quickly, and she was now carefully getting geared up for the tonight's meeting, making sure she left no *Jalissa* stone unturned. It felt like Halloween to Elissa because, whereby she and Jalissa physically looked like alike, they definitely had two different styles when it came to fashion.

Jalissa followed Elissa around the hotel room with her eyes as she watched this stranger transform into her. Jalissa didn't know what was going to become of this madness, but she prayed for the Lord to perform some type of miracle so this nightmare would go away and take this crazy lady with it.

Jalissa kept her eyes closed and continued to pray. Elissa checked her watch, which she'd retrieved from Jalissa's wrist, as well as her wedding band. It read 5:00 p.m. She took one last glance in the mirror and strutted out without saying one word to Jalissa. Jalissa really didn't know what was going on tonight, but Elissa had mentioned out loud that she had to hurry up and get to the church. Jalissa only assumed she meant her church. Jalissa had appeared to still be completely out of it, so Elissa resolved not to give her any more drugs. After tonight, everything would be over anyway, so she let Jalissa be, not knowing Jalissa wasn't as sedated as she had made Elissa believe. The effects of the morphine and the sleeping pill were wearing off. Jalissa knew it was nothing but the Lord who had made that possible. *God really does answer prayers*, she thought.

Jalissa wiggled her arms from side to side rapidly in hopes of loosening the duct tape and freeing herself. Each minute seemed like forever. She continued, and the tape wouldn't give. She'd almost given up hope until she heard a still, small voice in her head, urging her not to give up and to keep on trying. Jalissa found her second wind, and this time, she writhed and wiggled her entire body as if her life depended on it, and truthfully speaking, it did. The tape loosened, and Jalissa knew she had to keep trying.

Chapter Thirteen

Elissa parked her truck along the sidewalk near the side entrance of the church. She walked past a group of teens without acknowledging them.

"Oh, she just gonna walk by and don't speak," said one of the teenaged girls.

"Hmmm, y'all ain't read the community newsletter?" asked another girl.

"Nah, I ain't read the newsletter. Ain't nobody got time for that," responded one of the teenaged boys.

"Bottom line, First Lady is a phony," replied another.

"Another church phony...why am I not surprised?" another said sarcastically.

The group laughed and continued to mock *Jalissa*, or so they thought. Elissa started not to say anything since technically, they weren't talking about her, but the teens were so disrespectful, she couldn't let that slide. Elissa swiftly turned around and startled the teens. She knew they were startled when they all simultaneously paused and peered at her, wide-eyed.

"Let me tell y'all little rude, lack of home-training *children* something." She put emphasis on children. "Don't talk about things you know nothing about. Didn't your mothers teach you that children are to be seen and not heard?"

She turned around and strolled into the church. The teens were quiet until she was out of sight, then they started up with the insults again.

Once inside, Elissa smiled because, from that incident alone, it was obvious her plan was in motion. She'd already stripped Jalissa of her holy credibility. She poked her head inside the swinging doors to the sanctuary, but no one was there. She'd spotted a few vehicles parked in the back where the congregants parked, so she knew someone was in the building. The swinging doors swung closed on the hinges, and she continued down the hall, going nowhere in particular. Elissa eventually heard voices, which let her know she was headed in the

151

right direction. She stopped at the door with Pastor Jason Hill on the nameplate. Elissa started to feel nervous as she stood in front of the door, but there was no turning back now. She took a deep breath and prepared to give the best performance of her life. She lightly tapped on the door and entered upon being summoned.

Elissa humbly entered the room with her head lowered, the way she'd presumed Jalissa would have entered under these circumstances. There were several people in the office, but of course, she only recognized Jason. She greeted everyone in the room without mentioning names. She realized an older, prestigious gentleman in the room, sitting at Jason's cherry wood desk, and she assumed it was Bishop Martin, the head bishop. She took a gamble and greeted him personally, and thank God, she was correct in her assumption. She walked over to Jason and gave him a kiss on the cheek. She whispered in his ear that he'd better follow her lead if he had any sense. Jason shot her a quick glance laced with venom and hatred, but said nothing. Elissa took a seat next to him, and Bishop Martin wasted no time starting the meeting. He cleared his throat and started to speak.

"First Lady Hill, I'm not going to prolong this gathering. As you know, according to the organization bylaws, when it comes to situations of this magnitude, I need other members from the board to be present. That explains why Evangelist Dorothy and Bishop Gray are in attendance." The two nodded without saying a word.

Elissa could see the disgrace on their faces. Bishop continued.

"We're going to give you a chance to speak your peace, but then we have to make a final decision."

Bishop turned his attention to Jason, and his face softened. He apologized to him but clearly explained that there was a big chance the organization would have to replace him as pastor of the church, which would result in him and Jalissa being unemployed, and all benefits and perks revoked. Those perks included the luxury vehicles that both of them currently drove, and a combined yearly income of one hundred and twenty thousand dollars. Jason nodded, but still did not speak.

Bishop reached inside of his briefcase and spread the photos he'd received in the mail onto the desk. There were several with Elissa half-dressed, hanging on to some man with a drink in her hand, and another with her in the bed with a man. The man's bare chest was exposed, due to his arm being stretched out to take the photo. It was obvious they were naked under the covers. Then there were a few with Elissa in a hot tub, and a few more with her in a pool with different men. Elissa made sure to send the most explicit photos she could find from her college days.

"Can you explain these?" questioned the Bishop.

"Bishop, I respect you too much, so I will not waste your time, as well as the others." She nodded in the direction of the evangelist and the other Bishop. "First, I want to apologize to my husband and all of you for my lewd acts. Although those pictures were taken a few years ago, and in my younger days, it still doesn't eliminate the fact they were taken when I was married, and not to mention, that is not how a Christian and a first lady is expected to behave.

"It's only right that I also confess that I am having an affair with another man. I just can't live with the guilt any longer, so do what you have to do."

"I don't want to assume anything or misjudge the matter. I'm aware that with the fancy technology that is out these days, pictures can easily be altered, and photoshopped. So with that being said, are you admitting that this is actually you in these photos?"

"Yes, Bishop, I'm admitting that's me in the photos," Elissa mumbled with fake tears welling in her eyes.

The bishop turned his attention back to Jason and proceeded.

"Unfortunately, I hate to say this, but effective immediately, Pastor Hill, you are no longer pastor of this church. The organization can not allow you and your wife to continue as the leaders of this congregation, due to First Lady's tainted past, and her confession of a current affair. Yes, we all have done things we are ashamed of, but the fact that this information is so new and fresh, the organization feels the church would be greatly affected negatively, and we can't gamble the church's well-being. We must consider how people will react to this news because souls are our first priority."

Jason fidgeted in his seat until he couldn't take it anymore.

"She is a fraud!" Jason yelled, jumping up out of his chair and pointing at Elissa.

"Calm down, Pastor," implored the bishop. "I know you're upset, but unfortunately, these are the rules. You both need to be out by the end of this week."

"No, you're not hearing me. She's a fake, a phony. This is not my wife. This is not First Lady Jalissa."

Everyone stared at Jason as if he had lost his mind. Elissa peered at him as if to say, *Your wife is a dead woman.* Jason acknowledged her stare, but he didn't back down. He just couldn't take it anymore. He was counting on God to help him out of this situation since he knew this was all a lie.

"Look at her closely. This is not my wife," he continued to rant and rave.

Jason was hysterical at this point, and he felt he was having an out-of-body experience. Jason's main concern at this time wasn't him being excommunicated from his church, but his hysteria was because he didn't know what had become of his wife. He didn't know if she was hurt, or even alive for that matter, because it was clear that this woman, this imposter, his sister-in-law, was undoubtedly crazy. Jason continued his claim that the woman before them was not truly his wife. The bishop and the other attendees were speechless. No one said anything for a few moments while Jason went on and on.

"Pastor Jason, I understand this is difficult for you to accept, but—"

Jason cut the bishop off in the middle of his sentence.

"No disrespect, Bishop Martin, but nothing. This woman is *not* my wife." Jason bent down, leaned over, and pointed directly in Elissa's face as he continued his plea. He was now all up in Elissa's face, their noses almost touching. Elissa stared him directly in his eyes with a cold look and smirked, then forced tears to stream down her face. The room instantly broke out into chaos. Jason had never hit a woman in his life unless you counted Janet when he was in the third grade, and he'd only pushed her because he liked her.

Jason flipped out and grabbed Elissa by her neck. The chair she was sitting in toppled over, and

Jason was on top of her, squeezing as hard as he could. Evangelist Dorothy let out a screech and jumped to her feet. The two bishops rushed over to Jason, and it took both of them to get him off of Elissa. The two men held each one of Jason's arms, and Evangelist Dorothy tended to Elissa to make sure she wasn't hurt. Evangelist Dorothy didn't agree with the photos of the first lady, but she couldn't agree with Jason being violent toward her, either. Elissa gasped for air and held her neck. The two men had constrained Jason on the other side of the office. All three men were out of breath, and Jason was still yelling that this woman was not his wife.

"He's telling the truth," stated the person who had uninvitingly entered the office.

Jason looked up, and a feeling of relief swept over him. The woman's statement caused the room to go silent for a brief moment.

"I'm sorry, sister, but this is a private meeting."

"Oh no, Bishop, it's okay," replied Jason.

The bishop gazed at Jason with the obvious question on his face.

"She's my mother-in-law."

Jason had never been so happy to see someone in all his life. The blood drained from Elissa's face, and she became instantly weak. Good thing she was already sitting down because she didn't feel she could trust her legs to hold her up.

"Ann, w-wh-what are you doing here?" stuttered Elissa.

This situation was getting stranger by the minute. Ann extended an apologetic look toward Elissa, but she had to focus on the situation at hand. Earlier, when Ann had questioned Jason about Jalissa's whereabouts over the weekend, he lied and said she was at a women's church retreat. He hadn't revealed to his mother-in-law what was going on because he didn't want to risk Jalissa's safety, but now that she was there, what better person to clear up the fact that this was all a big misunderstanding and a case of mistaken identity?

Jason explained everything to Ann, and she asked to see the photos. Meanwhile, Elissa sat there paralyzed. She couldn't believe she'd known her biological mother all these years and Ann had never said a word.

Ann quietly analyzed the photos, holding each photo up closely as if she were looking for something specific. Her expression proved she couldn't find what she was looking for. Her eyebrows furrowed with each passing picture until she came across the photos taken in the pool and the hot tub. Ann let out a small sigh that didn't go unnoticed.

"Is there something in those pictures that prove it's not First Lady Jalissa?" asked the Bishop.

"Yes," replied Ann. "The woman in these photos is not First Lady Jalissa."

"How can you prove it?" questioned Evangelist Dorothy.

Ann briefly explained she'd given birth to identical twin daughters when she was a teenager, but there was one thing about them that made it easy to tell the two apart.

The office door opened once again and in walked Jalissa. Jason ran over to his wife and hugged her tightly as tears streamed down both their faces. After she'd freed herself in the hotel, she called her mother, and through uncontrollable tears, gave her a recap of her reunion with her twin sister. Ann broke numerous traffic laws to get to the hotel where Jalissa was. Everyone in the room was shocked, to say the least, by what was unfolding before their eyes. This was something you saw on television; the only things missing were snacks and drinks.

For the first time since she'd been abducted, Jalissa realized how much she and her abductor looked alike. It was eerie, even to her. Jalissa and Elissa stared at each other, each examining and admiring the other one's features.

"Okay, so it's clear that First Lady Jalissa has a twin, but how does that prove it isn't her in these compromising photos?"

"As I was saying, there is one distinct difference about them."

"And what is that?"

"One has a birthmark on her face, and one doesn't."

The bishop looked from one woman to the other. "I don't mean any disrespect, ma'am, but I'm looking at them, and I don't see a birthmark on either woman."

Ann walked over to the bishop and pointed out the birthmark on Elissa's face in the pool and hot tub photos. She then slowly walked over to Elissa and gently wiped her cheek with her hand. Tears streamed down Elissa's face, so the wetness made it easy for the makeup to be removed. Once the makeup was completely removed, a birthmark in the shape of a star appeared on Elissa's right cheek. The gentle, soft, loving touch of her mother seemed to take all the fight out of her. Elissa fell into Ann's arms and cried like a baby. Elissa no longer wanted revenge, she just wanted the love of her mother.

Ann held her with the same love she had for her when she held her that last time in the hospital before her aunt and uncle took her away. Jalissa and Jason looked on with tears in their eyes also and decided not to press charges. It didn't take a genius to understand she had reacted out of pain and rejection, and now was a perfect time for them both to practice what they preached, and that was forgiveness, no matter the circumstance.

Crystal Ann Johnson-McCoy apologized and explained everything to Elissa, and begged for her forgiveness. Elissa listened with an open heart as the tears continued to trickle down her face. Everything started to make sense. Her grandfather treated her mother the same way her great uncle had treated her. Ann expressed to Elissa that she'd never stopped loving her. She revealed she'd been following her for years and was very proud of her. When she couldn't take it anymore, she'd made it her business to introduce herself at the medical conference so she could stop watching her from a distance and become a part of her life, even if it was only as a friend.

Bishop Martin apologized to Jason and Jalissa and concluded he would explain to the board everything was a terrible misunderstanding. Bishop Martin and the other attendees left the office in order to give them privacy. It was clear it was definitely a case of mistaken identity, and their services were no longer required. First Lady Jalissa was innocent, and Jason would continue serving as senior pastor.

Chapter Fourteen
(It's Not Over)

Mr. Bradley hadn't seen Elissa in a few days, and he was starting to get worried. It wasn't common practice for him to keep tabs on the tenants in the buildings he worked in, but Elissa was different. He tended to his doorman duties but still couldn't shake the feeling of discomfort of not seeing his favorite tenant. She'd looked in his face day after day for years since he'd been working there, and not once had she noticed anything. Mr. Bradley didn't blame her, though; it was all her mother's fault.

Crystal had given birth and never said a word to him. She thought he didn't know she was carrying his baby, but her best friend Lisa couldn't keep her mouth shut for anything. She told him Crystal was pregnant by him. Lisa didn't know the whole story of what happened, so she felt it was okay to let him know. Lisa told him everything she knew about how Crystal was forced to give one of the babies away.

Rape or no rape, she was still carrying his child, and when he found out they were twins, he couldn't believe it. Sure, he wasn't in any position to take care of babies at that time, so he didn't make a big deal about it. He kept the information he received from Lisa stored in his head to be used at the opportune time. In the meantime, he earned an athletic scholarship, went to college, and became very successful.

Somehow, Crystal had vanished into thin air with one of his daughters, and he'd lost track of her, but he found Elissa and had been following her ever since in order to find Crystal. He'd hired the best in the business when it came to private investigating, and from the information he'd recently received, he was close.

He knew his son, Chance, was the best in the business. He stood outside the building in his uniform, peering up and down the street, seeing if

Elissa was approaching, but there were no signs of Elissa. *That's okay*, he thought, because the time had come for Crystal Ann Johnson to pay for keeping his children from him. Charles Bradley started plotting his revenge.

Be sure to LIKE our Major Key
Publishing page on Facebook!

CPSIA information can be obtained
at www.ICGtesting.com
Printed in the USA
LVHW031818100419
613666LV00004B/383